Praise for *Dark Wine at Christmas*

"This book is fun and light, a perfect Christmas story! I love how it focuses on the electric relationship between Cerissa, with her independent will, and Henry, who is struggling with his moral core. It reveals more of Rolf's rigid personality and the clever ways that Karen handles him. And the sparring between Henry and Rolf, the two dominant males—oh my goddess!"

~Shari Bonin-Pratt's Ink Flare

Also by Jenna Barwin

The Hill Vampire Series

DARK WINE AT THE ALTAR (BOOK 11)
Spring 2024

DARK WINE AT CHRISTMAS (BOOK 10)

DARK WINE AT DAWN (BOOK 9)

DARK WINE AT HALLOWEEN (BOOK 8)

DARK WINE AT THE GRAVE (BOOK 7)

DARK WINE AT DISASTER (BOOK 6)

DARK WINE AT THE CIRCUS (BOOK 5)

DARK WINE AT DEATH (BOOK 4)

DARK WINE AT DUSK (BOOK 3)

DARK WINE AT SUNRISE (BOOK 2)

DARK WINE AT MIDNIGHT (BOOK 1)

DARK WINE
AT
CHRISTMAS

A Hill Vampire Novel
Book 10

Jenna Barwin

Hidden Depths Publishing

Printed in the United States of America
First printing & ebook edition, 2023

Hidden Depths Publishing
Dana Point, California
www.hiddendepthspublishing.com

Cover design: Covers by Christian (Christian Bentulan)
Images used under license from Stock.adobe.com and Jacob Lund Photography ApS.
Cover art is for illustrative purposes only and any person depicted on the cover is a model or artist's creation.

Editing team: Katrina Diaz-Arnold, Refine Editing, LLC; Trenda K. Lundin, It's Your Story Content Editing; Arran McNicol, Editing 720.

Library of Congress Control Number: 2023913710

eBook ISBN 978-1-952755-13-2
Print 978-1-952755-14-9

1) Paranormal Romance 2) Urban Fantasy Romance 3) Vampire Romance 4) Vampire Mystery 5) Vampire Suspense 6) Paranormal Romantic Suspense 7) Romantic Fantasy

v1.0

Join Jenna Barwin's VIP Readers

Want to know about new releases, and receive special announcements, exclusive excerpts, and other FREE fun stuff?

Join Jenna's VIP Readers:
https://jennabarwin.com/jenna-barwins-newsletter/

You can also find Jenna Barwin on Facebook, TikTok, Twitter, and Instagram:
@JennaBarwin

Email: https://jennabarwin.com/contact

DARK WINE
AT
CHRISTMAS

CHAPTER 1
WITHOUT WARNING

La Guardia Airport, New York—Four days before Christmas

Enrique Bautista Vasquez—Henry to his close friends—was eager to reach Sierra Escondida a few hours before sunrise, and not just because he'd pass out at dawn. The three weeks he'd spent in New York City with his fiancée, Cerissa Patel, had provided enough time for the contractor to complete the surprise now awaiting her at their home: an early Christmas gift he was eager to show her.

While it was originally scheduled as a two-week vacation, they'd opted to extend their trip to New York by a week after several murders, two kidnappings, and the reappearance of an old foe had derailed their holiday—not to mention the recent drama caused by his maker, the woman who turned him vampire over two hundred years ago. But thanks to Cerissa's selflessness, he'd soon be free of Anne-Louise and her games once and for all.

After all the turmoil, the rest of the vacation had been a blessing. They took in all the theater performances Cerissa wanted to see, the restaurants she wanted to sample, and the tourist sights she wanted to visit. It was all topped off by the extravagant party Anne-Louise threw celebrating her sudden engagement to her mortal mate, NYPD detective Rick Fiorello.

The extra week of vacation was not only valuable for righting their trip, but for putting the finishing touches on his gift for Cerissa.

At La Guardia airport, light snow flurries surrounded the Dassault Falcon. The small jet's range would barely get them back to the Hill without dipping into the reserve tank. He hoped the weather wouldn't force them to land in Utah or Colorado to refuel.

He finished the final flight check waiting for the deicer to clear his windows. After receiving the tower's okay, he guided the plane down the tarmac for takeoff.

Once they were airborne, he switched to autopilot and asked, "Did you enjoy the engagement party last night?"

Someone had introduced Cerissa to chocolate martinis at the soirée. He'd poured her drunken, rubber-boned body into bed around four in the morning, tucked her in, and said goodnight without an opportunity to compare notes on the celebration.

"It was fun. I always love dancing with you."

"And you were the loveliest woman in the room."

She *tsked*. "You're biased."

Maybe he was. Still, she'd found the perfect dress while shopping in the city and easily outshined the bride-to-be.

"Anne-Louise looked gorgeous, and Rick seemed contented," Cerissa added. "I was happy to see those two back together."

After Anne-Louise and Rick announced their engagement, Cerissa forgave the arm-twisting method Anne-Louise employed to get a taste of Cerissa's blood and determine her mortality. Whatever hard feelings she might have carried were truly gone, and the ladies had returned to their usual good-natured banter.

Henry *harrumphed* and glanced at the controls, making sure all was well. "You have a bigger heart than I do."

She squeezed his thigh. "Your heart is fine. You just have a longer and rockier history with your maker than I do. It's easier for me to step back and view events objectively."

If only he could so easily forgive his maker. Thus far, his rage hadn't abated, and the fire was still smoldering. But then, for over two centuries he'd been burning with resentment toward the woman who'd robbed him of his mortal life.

But forgiveness came naturally to Cerissa. She recognized Anne-Louise's motivation had been to protect Henry from a perceived threat, which came a little too close to the truth. Although Cerissa represented no threat to his well-being, Anne-Louise was right about one thing: Cerissa wasn't mortal. She was part of the Alatus Lux—something they both worked diligently on to keep secret, even though there had been a few oops moments.

"At least Anne-Louise learned nothing from the bite."

"Indeed." Henry raised her hand to his lips and kissed the soft skin sensually. "Your secret is safe."

"Except from Tig. Have you heard anything further from her?"

"*Querida*, stop worrying. Tig won't say anything about you, except to Jayden. Relax. Enjoy the flight."

"And you—relax and enjoy being free from Anne-Louise."

"I will try."

"Good." She smiled mischievously at him. "Can I take the controls and get some flight time on our way home?"

Cerissa had been training for her pilot's license by studying manuals and running simulation tests. In addition, she needed to log pilot hours to qualify.

"Didn't you have a drink at dinner?"

"Hair of the dog. Those martinis were good, but potent." She laughed, holding up her index finger. "I had one martini—just one—when I ate my chicken alfredo, and with my metabolism—"

"No. Even if you think you're fine, you should wait the requisite time, just as mortals do. I'll find another opportunity for you to pilot."

"I guess." She shrugged. "Then I'll sleep while you keep us in the air. Or we could talk about our own wedding plans."

"Too distracting. We'll find time when I'm not piloting." Or, at least, when he didn't need to monitor the autopilot. And if he was honest with himself, he wasn't looking forward to the disagreements that inevitably arose when planning an occasion as special as their wedding.

"Hmm." The cabin's heater had warmed the small space, and she removed the cute fake fur hat she'd worn in New York to protect her head from the cold. The way she raked her fingers through the long mink-brown hair made him envision how her hair fanned across his pillow. With a thoughtful expression on her face, she finally said, "You're just hoping I'll make all the wedding decisions so you don't have to."

"*Querida,* when have you ever known me to delegate control to anyone?"

"If you put it that way—"

He squeezed her hand. "I want our wedding to be special too, something we'll remember forever."

"Then we'll sit down and start going over details soon?"

"Of course." He couldn't put it off forever. "We've already picked October—"

"But not the date—"

"We will soon." He suppressed a groan. Maybe he did want her to make all the decisions, as contrary as that would be. "After the holidays, we can start planning in earnest."

"Fine. But my family is still paying for the wedding."

"As we agreed."

"And I'll pay for the honeymoon."

"What?" Did she think he couldn't afford what she wanted? Yes, money was tight, but he'd find a way to raise the funds for the honeymoon she desired. "On the Hill, it's traditional for the vampire to pay."

"I don't care. You're paying for all our living expenses—our housing, food, clothing. What am I supposed to do with my income?"

"Indulge yourself when you want and invest the rest."

"*Henry.*" Her emerald eyes pierced him.

He made a sweeping gesture at the cockpit window. "Now is not the time to argue the matter. I'm piloting."

"You mean the autopilot is piloting?"

"Conceded. But we should discuss this when I'm not distracted."

Cerissa fell silent, and he glanced over at her. She was biting her lip, her brow furrowed.

He swung his gaze back to the instrument panel. "We need to agree upon a budget for the wedding and honeymoon—"

"I won't know how much to budget until we make some decisions, Henry. The venue for the sangeet party—you can't forget that—"

"You've mentioned the sangeet on prior occasions. What is it?"

"When our families come together the day before the wedding to celebrate and dance and sing. A big pre-wedding party, but for family. In our case, the people we've chosen as family, like Karen and Rolf."

"I see."

"And, of course, there's the location of the wedding, and the number of guests, and where we'll go on our honeymoon. You know—the basics. All those affect the budget."

"I'll consider your request to *share* the honeymoon expense." He'd never let her pay for the entire trip. "We can discuss this after the holidays."

"All right." Cerissa leaned her chair back and closed her eyes. "In that case, I'm going to nap."

Henry claimed her hand and pressed his lips to her palm. "Sweet dreams," he said, returning her hand to her lap.

Half-lidded, she studied him with a begrudging smile, then shut her eyes.

Shortly before landing at Sierra Escondida Municipal Airport, he woke her and couldn't help the gleeful grin gracing his face. Cerissa's glance asked why he was so excited—but he just shook his head. She'd have to wait until they arrived home to learn what was in store for her. After which, he hoped there'd be at least an hour remaining before dawn to spend in bed with her, where perhaps she could show her gratitude for his generosity.

Despite their being equal partners, he occasionally enjoyed indulging his sugar daddy fantasy when it was his turn to choose their bedroom activities. And his wonderful mate played along beautifully—in the bedroom.

Not so much outside of it.

Unloading their luggage went quickly, and they didn't have to wait for a ride, as he'd stored their car in the airport hangar reserved for his plane. A short drive later, they passed the guarded gates of the exclusive town of Sierra Escondida. The Central California town was ensconced in a picturesque hillside valley of vineyards, and home to a community of vampires and their mortal mates. He made a left onto the curving driveway leading to their Spanish colonial residence—white, smooth stucco and terracotta tiles.

After parking in the garage, he rolled the bags across the cobblestones to the front porch of their home, disengaged the alarm using his phone, and then unlocked the door. Why did the foyer still smell of carpentry? The contractor had assured him the project would be finished by now.

He carried in the heavier luggage, and she followed with her small roller suitcase. "What is that scent?" She sniffed at the air. "Fresh pine wood and...fresh paint?"

"Two surprises for you." He closed the front door after her. "Leave your bag here and come with me."

Taking her hand, he led her to the doors of the drawing room and threw them open. In the corner near the fireplace, a tall Christmas tree filled the space where a table and armchairs normally sat. Fully decorated in gold globes, twinkling white lights, and a glitter-covered star, the tree shimmered.

"Oh, Henry, it's gorgeous!" Then her face fell into a slightly distressed expression. "But I thought we'd decorate our first tree together."

He slid his arms around her and brought her lips to his. When their gentle kiss ended, he whispered, "Next year we'll decorate our own tree. With Christmas so close now, I didn't want you to feel rushed."

She relaxed in his arms. "That makes sense. Thank you, truly. But next year, we'll do this together. Promise?"

He nodded. "Of course, *querida*." He wove his fingers through hers. "Now for the second surprise. Come upstairs with me."

Once they were upstairs, he whipped out a blindfold he'd stuffed in his pocket before leaving New York.

"What is that for?"

They'd experimented with blindfolds and bondage in the bedroom before, and he could scent her arousal and feel the shiver of her excitement through the crystal.

He chuckled. "Not what you are imagining."

Although after the surprise, maybe.

Once he placed the blindfold over her eyes and tied the string, he firmly clasped her arm and guided her down the hallway, past her bedroom, past his office, halting at the door of the former storage room. Over the years, he'd purchased many original oil paintings, too many to hang on his walls. The space between his office and the media room had held the overflow for close to a century in an environment controlled for humidity and temperature. Occasionally, he rotated the paintings he hung in the foyer and drawing room with the ones in storage to mix things up.

Opening the door, he led her inside and untied the blindfold. "Voilà!"

She blinked rapidly, probably clearing her vision, and then exclaimed, "Oh, Henry, this is lovely. Is this—"

"Yes, your office. I promised it months ago, and had the work done while we vacationed. Do you like it?"

"Absolutely." She moved to the drafting table—the type architects used. He'd included the oversized, tiltable table because he'd observed how she spread out documents on a flat surface when working, usually the dining room table. "This is perfect."

"I am glad you like it."

Next, she stepped over to the executive desk and computer table and sat in the cushy chair, facing the opposite wall where a couch was positioned.

The interior designer had purchased a modern Scandinavian-style couch with zippered slipcovers in a leopard pattern. Cerissa could change them whenever she wanted to and even catch a catnap on the couch in cougar form, then wash the cushion covers to clean off her fur—not that the interior designer knew that part.

Cerissa leaned back in the ergonomic executive chair. "Comfy." Then she ran her fingers over the hardwood desk. "But can we afford it all?"

"The expense is taken care of. Do not worry."

"But I do worry. We're a team."

They'd been on a tighter budget and had originally agreed that the vacation to New York would be their mutual Christmas gifts to each other.

"I managed to eke out some extra funds from the artwork I sold. Paintings by Méi that I no longer enjoy as much as others. The art conservator removed the oil paintings during the time we were gone and transported them to a fire-safe building specifically designed for conserving and storing artwork. The two I sold paid for long-term storage and the room renovation."

"I don't know what to say." Cerissa stood and turned around. "This must have cost a lot to do."

He loved her. She was more than worth it. "Open the supply closet."

With a lift of her brow, she gripped the knob and went inside, disappearing from his view. "Oh my Goddess."

It was a walk-in closet with shelves that would allow her to keep paper and other supplies close at hand, but in perfect order. Cerissa veered toward being messy in her spaces, but the meticulous organizer in him couldn't help but provide her with the option, should she be inclined to use it. When she returned still looking happily stunned, her eyes lit on the French door connecting their offices, on the tiny windowpanes allowing her to see his desk.

"You have often said that you want to spend more time together. This way, we are a very short distance from each other, even when working."

She wrapped her arms around his neck. "Thank you, Henry. This is just so wonderful."

"Merry Christmas, *cariña*."

"But you cheated. We weren't supposed to get each other gifts. The vacation—"

He touched his index finger to her lips. "And what did you call the daylight bracelet? An early Christmas present?"

In New York, Cerissa had given him one of the greatest gifts of his long life. The Alatus Lux engineers had created a device, worn on his wrist, that protected him from the sun. It allowed him to see the sunrise and move about in open daylight for the first time in two centuries. It was quite the Christmas gift.

"I guess I did. But really, the daylight bracelet could be your birthday present." She gave him a quick kiss and plopped onto the couch. Pulling on his hand, she encouraged him to join her. "Your birthday is today. Is there anything special you want to do when you wake tonight?"

He sat next to her. "December twenty-first is not my birthday."

"But your driver's license says it is."

His lips quirked up. She must have sneaked a peek without him realizing it. So many things to learn about each other—they'd never exchanged actual birth dates. Or if they had, she had forgotten. "I picked December twenty-first for my last birth certificate because it's convenient. It's the longest night of the year. If I use that date, I have a better chance of being awake when the Department of Motor Vehicles is open. On the

Hill, December is a popular month for birthdays. I'm surprised some nosy statistician never noticed the trend."

"Clever. So when is your actual birthday?"

"It is unimportant."

"Unimportant? It's the day you were born. I want to celebrate it with you."

"So, which day matters the most?" He captured her hand. "The day I was born mortal or the day I was born vampire?"

"Which would you prefer to celebrate?"

"Neither. I would rather celebrate the day I first made love to you."

That date was easy to remember. Eight months ago, on the night of the spring dance, he'd brought her home with him, started his seduction under the stars, and finished in the pool house bed.

She gave him a cockeyed grin and shook her head. "You do love to win, don't you?"

"Yes, I do."

"Well, I can hardly get angry with you after receiving this wonderful gift."

"That is good, because I have something to ask you."

"What is that, Henry?"

"Will you go with me to Christmas mass? Father Matt will officiate at the midnight mass on *Nochebuena*. I would like it very much if you were at my side."

"I would be honored to go with you. Will it be a Catholic service?"

"Not really. It is nondenominational because we are such a small community. But I enjoy it nonetheless, and will enjoy it even more if I can share it with you."

"Of course, Quique. Are there any other ways you celebrate Christmas?"

"When I was a young man, we would have a feast before mass, which included homemade tamales. If you and Karen and some others want to put together a dinner, that would be fine."

"I'll talk with her about it. But you should clue me in if there are particular traditions that you follow, since this is our first holiday together."

"I will consider it. The mass is what I look forward to most."

"All right. But you will not avoid telling me your actual birth date by changing the topic."

"I was hoping you wouldn't notice."

He snaked an arm around her and snuggled her closer until her head rested against his chest. *Hmm.* The washable covers would allow them to do other romantic things on the couch.

"Please tell me." She tilted her head back, smiling at him.

"I was born in April and turned in mid-August. That will have to do for now. If I gave you the precise dates, you might do something I don't want you to."

"Like celebrate your birthday? Or cast your astrology chart?"

"Exactly." Then it sank in. "Wait. Astrology?"

She tapped her chin. "Aries and Leo. Two fire signs. I should have guessed. But I always tagged you for a Taurus. Bull-headed and broody, with anger issues."

Did she just insult him? Maybe. Yet he had to admit the high-altitude view was fairly accurate. Still. "Please tell me you don't believe in astrology."

"Vedic astrology is still big in India—it's different from American astrology. I grew up with the Vedic version."

"I'm going to regret asking this, but how is it different?"

"Western astrology was set two thousand years ago and hasn't changed. Since then, because the earth wobbles a bit when it spins, the relationship to the other planets changes, and the position of the sun and planets in relation to the signs no longer match. Vedic astrology calculates horoscopes based on the updated ecliptic path."

He groaned. He loved *astronomy*, observing the planets move in their courses, so he instantly understood the wobble—known as a precession—and its effect on the earth's journey. But *astrology*? No. Just no.

She smirked. "You're already aware I read women's magazines, to get a sense of portraying a woman in this modern age, so I'm familiar with the American version, even though it's out of date."

"You read the astrology columns." He said it as a statement, not a question, and groaned again.

"And the advice columns," she said brightly. "They help me understand this culture better."

He ignored her last comment. How could she learn anything from the drama in the agony columns? "You know astrology isn't scientifically accurate. Not even Vedic astrology."

"Of course. But it's fun."

"Then I am definitely not giving you the dates."

"I'd need your time of birth, too, to cast an accurate chart. But I can wait. At least I've learned a bit more about you since the evening started. Besides, I can always call Anne-Louise and ask her the date she turned you."

"I doubt she remembers."

Cerissa eyed him seductively. "I would remember the date if I were your maker."

"That's because you're a romantic," he said, leaning over and kissing her. "But just in case she does remember, I forbid you to ask her."

"I don't believe you have the power to forbid me from doing anything."

He sighed. She was absolutely right. He'd made it sound like an order, something he knew better than to do. "Very well. Allow me to rephrase. I would appreciate it very much if you wouldn't ask her. I will tell you when I am ready."

"When you put it that way, Quique, I'll wait." She smiled, a twinkle in her eyes. "For now."

CHAPTER 2

FRIENDS ARE FAMILY

ROLF AND KAREN'S HOME—DECEMBER 24

On Christmas Eve, Cerissa carried one tray of tamales, and Henry the other. They walked across the driveway and approached Rolf and Karen's front door, where a lush evergreen wreath hung, tied about with holly and stiff gold ribbon.

The night before, three other couples had joined her and Henry for *la tamalada*—a tamale-making assembly line that he created in the kitchen and supervised. Christine and Zeke were there, as were Marcus and Nicholas—and, to Cerissa's surprise, Henry had also invited Tig and Jayden.

The deal: they would split equally the total number of tamales made, and she and Henry would bring their share to the impromptu holiday party Karen and Rolf had agreed to host.

Henry spent the prior night doing all the prep work for *la tamalada*—slicing, dicing, and simmering the tasty fillings. Rich aromas had filled the kitchen and smelled like home, even though the spices he cooked with differed from those used by the women in her childhood home in India. It was the love with which he mixed the chile ancho, cumin, and other Mexican spices that imparted the aura of being home.

On the night of *la tamalada*, with Christmas music playing, they formed two assembly lines on each side of the kitchen island. The first person lined a corn husk with masa dough, made from ground corn hominy. They handed the husk to the next person, who added a meat or vegetarian filling. Then the last person in line folded the whole piece together and tied off the husk.

The mortals on the assembly line enjoyed eggnog with rum, and Cerissa had offered alcohol-spiked blood to the vampires. Then the assembly line created tamale after tamale as they joked and laughed and told stories about their lives.

Henry steamed some of the first tamales they produced and cut them into pieces for taste testing. Cerissa popped one of those in her mouth and moaned as the soft, steamed masa melted around the spicy, tender pork. Nicholas praised them so highly that Christine even tried a bite, then ran to the sink to spit it out. "How come they smell so good but taste awful?" she asked, then rinsed her mouth with water.

Zeke sidled up to her. "'Cause you're a new vampire. Your smeller's still set for mortal foods, but your taste buds only cotton to blood."

Cerissa giggled. Even Henry laughed at Zeke's comments, despite how seriously he approached the tamale-making process.

A warm feeling of belonging—something she wasn't accustomed to—had enveloped her. Together with their friends, she enjoyed the work and camaraderie of tamale making, and something settled in her. In the past, she'd never been in one place long enough to make deep friendships.

And now she had. Christine, Zeke, Marcus, and Nicholas all treated her as a friend and an equal.

Except one small thing nagged at her. Throughout *la tamalada*, she'd caught the significant looks and whispers between Tig and Jayden. Given the digs Tig had taken at her in New York after inadvertently discovering Cerissa was Lux, she'd avoided being alone with the chief of police. She wasn't sure how Tig felt about her. Or how Jayden felt now that Tig had filled him in.

During their ordeals in New York, Cerissa had made the mistake of bringing some of the Cutter's henchmen to the Lux Enclave. Tig had defended Cerissa in front of Agathe, gotten right in the Lux leader's face when she threatened to confine Cerissa and Ari to the Enclave. It was a really gutsy move on Tig's part. Cerissa knew she'd have to approach the chief sometime to ensure all was well.

But aside from the looks and whispers exchanged between Tig and Jayden during their tamale making, they acted as if nothing had happened.

The uncertainty of it all made Cerissa cautious and curious. They couldn't talk openly, since the other guests present weren't in on the secret, so it gave her an excuse to procrastinate—because she wasn't ready to check in yet.

On Christmas Eve, when she arrived at the front porch to Karen and Rolf's house, her thoughts still swirled with questions over what Tig and Jayden's interactions meant. Climbing the steps, Cerissa registered a different threat and glanced down at the tamale tray she carried to ensure she held it well away from the glittery fuchsia fabric of her cocktail dress. She didn't want to start the evening with tamale juice staining the skirt. She'd purchased the fancy attire in New York and had relished a reason to wear it with her smoky-eyed party makeup.

Assured her dress was safe, she looked over at Henry. He was dashing in a black suit with a scarlet crewneck underneath. Rather than his typical white starched shirt and tie, he wore his gold crucifix over the silk knit sweater. His long ebony hair was gathered into a sleek ponytail and tied back with a black satin ribbon.

How was she going to keep her hands off him for the next three hours? He looked so luscious and smelled equally appetizing. The spicy scent of his cologne—clove, cedar, and other earthy scents—tickled her nose, enticing her to jump his bones.

With all the vacation sex they'd had, she thought they might need a break. The truth was just the opposite. She couldn't get enough of him.

On the tail of that thought, the front door opened. Cerissa's legs propelled her into the foyer, her face heated with embarrassment, and she tried to stop thinking about Henry naked.

After exchanging air kisses and dress compliments with Karen, Cerissa said, "Your house is beautifully decorated."

"Thanks, bestie. I had help. Rolf didn't give me much notice that we were throwing a party tonight. I had to call in reinforcements."

"That may be our fault. The dinner was Henry's idea."

"Don't worry. I'm having fun with it. I love hosting."

Cerissa stopped in front of a flocked, traditional tree sitting in the foyer to "ooh" and "aah" over it. Red and white ornaments hung from the evergreen branches, and silver garland and lights wrapped around each bough. The sight was magical.

"Wait until you see the second one," Karen said, taking the tamales from Cerissa and tilting her head toward the living room. "Go get yourself a drink. Wine bar is that way. I'll find you after I place these on the buffet."

Hurrying, Karen disappeared through the dining room arch, and Henry followed with the tray he carried. Cerissa went into the living room, where the second tree, an even taller one, stood. It was hung with unique ornaments Karen had collected over the years, including about twenty mermen—sexy, shirtless guys with mermaid tails, each representing a different profession or place of origin. They'd discussed Karen's collection on the phone, but seeing it on display was quite impressive.

The veterinarian merman caught her eye. He wore a doctor's coat with each of his arms wrapped around a puppy. So cute. The ornament reminded her of Rolf's German shepherds—Karen had mentioned taking them to the vet while Cerissa was in New York. She'd meant to follow up and ask how they were doing.

Turning away from the tree, she scanned the living room, looking for friendly faces, and her fingers tightened over the thin strap of her evening purse. No one she called a friend was in sight.

Twice the size of Henry's drawing room, the elegant, marble-tiled space felt cold and hard, matching the mean vampires filling it. To her left stood Mitchell, who regularly mansplained to women in general and had been nasty to her in particular when she first arrived, even though Cerissa befriended his mate, Aeesha. Other vampires clustered to Cerissa's right, such as Nellie Wadsworth and Rose Haber. Those two feared strangers and expressed it with a level of snark and dark, snarling façades that communicated their distrust.

Cobras to the left of me, mambas to the right.

She had been on the receiving end of cutting remarks during previous encounters with the same vampires—many of whom felt they were superior to mortals—and her experience with them left her unsure what to do.

Then she spotted Tig and Jayden and breathed a light sigh. Crossing the room, weaving her way through the tall, linen-covered cocktail tables—the regular furniture had been removed to create an area for mingling—Cerissa suddenly realized who surrounded her friends, and her hand involuntarily rolled into a tight fist. Vishon Bathory and other vampires, the ones who'd spewed all kinds of nastiness when Olivia framed Cerissa for the former mayor's murder, were chatting with Tig and Jayden. She wasn't sure she'd ever get over being publicly shamed by them, not enough to socialize with her accusers.

Why did Rolf have to invite them? Despite his sarcastic ways and his initial attempts to get her chucked off the Hill, he'd accepted her as a friend and ally. So, who were these people? His political base? He made no secret that he wanted to be re-elected as mayor. And if she recalled correctly, his main constituency had consisted of vampires who distrusted mortals.

Maybe she shouldn't take his choice of guests so personally.

She veered off and went straight to the bartender and asked for a glass of Cabernet, trying to steer clear of the prickly crowd. Standing at the gathering's edge, she took two long sips of her wine to calm her nerves.

It didn't help.

As her discomfort grew, Henry came up behind her, one hand on her back. His light touch reassured her. "I'm right here, Cerissa." he said, rolling the R in her name the way she loved hearing it. "We are meant to have fun tonight. I'll stay by your side until you feel better."

The crystal embedded in his wrist connected their emotions and must have communicated her anxiety. "Thanks, Henry."

She sipped her drink and watched Karen work her way through the room, greeting people but never staying in one place too long. When Karen reached them, she caught Cerissa's arm. "Hey, girlfriend. I could use some help in the kitchen. Want to come with me?"

"Gladly." Cerissa accepted a kiss on the cheek from her mate and smiled at him. "I'll be fine. Go talk with your friends."

He sketched a bow, and she accompanied her bestie into the kitchen. "What can I do to help?"

"Have a seat and keep me company."

Cerissa pulled out one of the low-backed highchairs at the kitchen island and placed her wineglass on the granite top with a *clink*, then played with the stem nervously.

Karen removed another tray of sliced ham from the oven and set it on a pretty gray and white trivet. "So, when are we getting together? I've hardly seen you since Thanksgiving."

"True, but I'm free tomorrow."

"Perfect! Let's have Christmas lunch here. We're going to have a ton of leftovers." Karen laughed as she transferred the warmed ham to a holiday-themed platter.

"Sure, that sounds like a great idea."

"And maybe you can tell me what happened in New York."

"Yeah, maybe."

Karen cocked her head to one side. "What's bugging you, girlfriend?"

"Ah... Well..."

Laying aside the serving fork, Karen came around the island and gave Cerissa a hug. "Please remember: any time you need to talk, I'm here for you."

Cerissa returned the hug, trying to shake off her nerves. "I know. It's just that there are so many people here."

"Especially those who were nasty over the whole Olivia thing, right?"

"How did you guess?"

"Doesn't take a brain scientist. I told Rolf to go easy on the guestlist, but he wouldn't listen."

"I'll be all right, I think."

When Karen eased back from the hug, she hooked her pinky around a strand of auburn hair, tucked it behind an ear, and moved to the sink to wash her hands. "I better get the ham served before the hungry horde hunts me down."

Karen resumed placing slices on the platter. The black, shimmery dress she wore looked perfect on her, though the holiday apron she'd temporarily tied around her waist sort of ruined the effect.

Suddenly, Cerissa felt two hands squeeze her shoulders from behind, one on each side. Her heart went into overdrive, and she spun around to see who it was.

Tig.

"Why is Henry's little angel hiding in the kitchen with our hostess?"

Karen coughed and gazed askance at Tig.

"My little *angelito* is helping her best friend," Henry said, as he walked into the kitchen and circled an arm around Cerissa's back. Tig let go of Cerissa's shoulders, shifting to her left to accommodate him.

"In all truth?" Cerissa said, letting the sadness creep into her voice. "I don't want to be near those people, the ones who said such awful things at the hearing. When we were at the Halloween party, there was more space. It was easier to ignore them. Here, it's closer quarters. I can't avoid them if I return to the living room."

"What you should do is simple." Tig squeezed her left shoulder again. "Look them straight in the eye and don't let them steal your victory. You won. The town council fully cleared your name. Your research lab is being built as we speak. You helped me capture the Carlyle Cutter. You are worth ten times one of those noisemakers."

"Really?"

Tig nodded at her. "Really."

Warmth fluttered through Cerissa. So it hadn't been all show when Tig defended her to Agathe. Tig accepted what she was. Valued it.

"And why are you in the kitchen?" Henry asked Tig.

The chief shrugged. "Besides learning why your little angel slunk from the room?"

Karen's gaze bounced from Tig to Henry to Cerissa with a tinge of panic this time.

"Relax," Cerissa said. "Tig knows. I'll tell you the entire story tomorrow over lunch."

"Oh." Karen blinked rapidly, twice. She gripped her wineglass and took a deep swig. "Okay."

Cerissa bit back a giggle. Yes, that was awkward. She'd wanted to tell Karen in person but had lacked the opportunity before now.

Henry slewed his eyes in Tig's direction. "And you're in the kitchen because...?"

"The wine bar is low on Cabernet. Jayden suggested I find our hostess and tell her. He was engrossed in his conversation with Councilmember Vishon about the latest comic book he bought."

Vishon was already on Cerissa's "mean vampire" list. But if her evaluation of him was correct, why did he pretend to be nice when speaking to Jayden? Did having hobbies in common overcome his attitude toward mortals?

"Gotcha." Karen went into the wine pantry, returned carrying four bottles of Cabernet, and handed them to Tig and Henry to deliver to the wine bar.

Before Tig could leave, Cerissa stiffened her backbone and asked the question bugging her. "How is Jayden taking the news? About me?"

Tig snorted. "I think his comic book hobby made it easier for him to, ah, believe the truth—but he's still processing it all. Maybe you can ask him to join you and Karen for lunch and talk to him, put his mind to rest."

"Consider the invitation extended. We'll meet at Karen's. She has all the leftovers."

"Make it your house," Karen said. "I'll bring the food, but this place will be a wreck tomorrow. I'm not staying up all night to clean."

Cerissa mentally surveyed her house. The kitchen was spotless, and the wrapping paper she and Henry had left on the floor in the drawing room could be swept away in a minute. Karen's plan worked. "Done deal."

"I'll tell Jayden to join you at noon."

"Why is everyone in here?" Rolf asked, striding into the room and dropping off an empty platter.

Tig shot him a disapproving look. "Because you've been avoiding me." Her lips tightened. "We need to discuss certain information that came to my attention in New York—"

"*Ach.* Give it a rest. We can talk after the holidays. I'm on vacation for the next few weeks. No town council business. None."

Cerissa snickered. She'd love to be a fly on the wall for that chewing out. Not that Tig had any room to complain now that she'd been sworn to secrecy about the Lux.

"Just tell me," Tig replied. "Are you keeping anything else from me?"

Karen's gaze scanned all of them. "And I want to know why no one told me she knows."

"*Liebling*, I'm sorry," Rolf said, taking her into his arms. "I didn't want to upset you. Tig and I will talk after our vacation." Letting Karen go, he added in Tig's direction, "*Mein Gott*, it's nothing urgent." He clapped his hands. "Everyone, back to the party. Now."

With a cocky grin, Henry waved at the archway leading to the living room. "After you."

"I'll finish helping Karen," Cerissa replied.

Once Tig, Henry, and Rolf left, Karen said, "You should have warned me."

"I never expected her to say anything to you. I was hoping to tell you all the deets in person tomorrow. It's not something I wanted to discuss over the phone, especially because it involved the Carlyle Cutter. I wasn't sure if hearing about him would be triggering."

"Yeah, right. You just enjoyed seeing me gape at you like a carp." Karen lifted the platter of ham from the kitchen island. "And as far as the Cutter goes, Rolf told me he's dead, and I'm fine with it. Now grab that tray and follow me."

Using potholders, Cerissa carried the sweet potato casserole and followed Karen. "Where are Mort and Sang?"

Karen laughed. "Enjoying their Christmas dinner in the dog run outside. You wouldn't want them in here. They'd slobber on your pretty plum dress, and get you and everyone else covered in fur."

Cerissa smiled. Yes, the dogs could be messy in their enthusiasm when greeting her after a long absence, but she wouldn't mind sacrificing her outfit to see them. She set the casserole dish on the huge dining room table, which was overflowing with food.

"Are they okay? You mentioned a vet visit—"

"They are just fine. Quit fretting."

"Maybe we can go say hello to the dogs before we leave." She loved them, and something about the German shepherds calmed her nerves.

"There is no time," Henry said from behind her. He put his hands on her hips and turned her to him for a kiss. "You should eat now. We leave for *Nochebuena* services in an hour."

She checked her watch. There was plenty of time to eat and socialize. They didn't need to hurry. But knowing Henry, he probably wanted to arrive early to get a seat in the first few rows.

After services, would he have any more surprises up his sleeve? He'd bought her a sexy peignoir set. If she had to guess, the next surprise would be him naked under the Christmas tree.

A scorching blush flooded her cheeks. She really had to stop reading those smutty romance novels. Now, she couldn't shake the image of how stunning he'd look, and a pleasant heat ran between her legs. Her mind kept envisaging all sorts of fun things they could do on a sheepskin rug by the fireplace.

He grinned at her evilly. *Damn.* He could probably smell her arousal. How could she now go to church thrumming with sexual desire?

She sighed, forcing herself to focus on the dogs rather than a naked Henry. Maybe she could sneak a peek at Mort and Sang before leaving. But then she recalled it'd rained during the day. She didn't want to track mud into the Viper—he'd have a fit. No, she'd wait until tomorrow to visit them, because tonight, she was all Henry's.

Chapter 3

CELEBRATING

Rancho Bautista del Murciélago—After chapel services

Henry helped Cerissa remove her coat, kissing her cheek as he did. "What would you enjoy doing now, *mi amor*?"

His vampire child, Christine, was spending the night with Zeke, so they had the house all to themselves. No one would disturb them.

She tapped a finger on her lips. "I have an idea. Why don't you go upstairs, undress completely, but put on your robe? I'll text you when I'm ready for you."

He'd noticed the delightful aroma of arousal emanating from her earlier, and as they stood in the foyer, the warm scent rose stronger, mingling with her Chanel No. 5 perfume. "But it's my turn to choose," he replied.

They had agreed to take turns leading. Two nights ago, she'd driven their lovemaking, deciding what they did in bed—or in the shower, or on the kitchen table, or just about anywhere in the house. The key point was they traded off who led when they made love, mainly so he wouldn't dominate all the time, and so she had space to express her desires.

She grinned slyly. "Trust me, you won't be disappointed."

It was Christmas Eve. Why not be spontaneous and indulge whatever whim she had in mind?

Her arms went around his neck, and she pulled him close for a deep kiss, her body pressed firmly against his. That was all it took for him to grow hard.

She lowered a hand and squeezed his *pene* through his pants. "Take your time. I need to get things ready."

That made him even harder. She had something planned, and he couldn't wait to discover what. After bowing to her, he went upstairs and did as she requested. He put his clothes away, hanging what could be worn again, throwing into the hamper what couldn't. Once completely naked, he slipped on his robe, which resembled an old-fashioned knee-length smoking jacket, and felt awkward moving while tenting the brocade fabric. Then he untied the satin ribbon holding back his ponytail, leaving his hair loose the way she preferred it.

On an impulse, he wrapped the ribbon around his *pene* and tied it loosely into an ostentatious bow. Something he'd read had put the image in his mind.

When the text message arrived, he rushed back downstairs to the drawing room, per her instructions. "*Querida, magnífico!*"

The lights to the Christmas tree were on, a roaring fire filled the fireplace, and the rest of the room was dark. In front of the hearth, she'd made a nest from pillows, blankets, and the thick sheepskin rug that normally lay in front of his listening chair on the hardwood floor in his music library. Standing in the center, she wore the special present he'd bought her, although she'd accused him of buying the gift for himself.

The dark magenta G-string with a grapevine appliqué wrapped over her mound, the string dipping between her thighs and back over her hips. The matching bra, the cups and halter also sewn with a solid grapevine appliqué, covered her nipples but left a lot of lush sienna-brown skin visible.

He tented the robe even more.

She gestured at the wineglasses on the fireplace hearth. "Alcohol-infused blood for you, wine for me. You didn't get to partake at the party, since you were driving. I thought you might like to unwind."

He hadn't noticed the refreshments, as he'd locked his gaze solely on her. Ignoring the drinks, he eased her into his arms and let one hand drift to her thigh; his fingers slid underneath the small patch of vines to finger her clit and run slow circles over it. She was already sopping wet, and his *pene* pulsed in response. He pressed his fingers on to her clit a little more firmly, and she moaned against his throat. The sound vibrated his skin.

"Come for me, *querida*. Standing here, just like this. I've wanted to touch you all night. I cannot wait any longer."

"Oh my Goddess," she murmured as her back arched, and he bent forward to take a nipple into his mouth through the woven vine, sucking hard, never stopping his fingers.

"Come for me," he said, his mouth still hovering over her breast, letting the warmth of his breath pass across the wet nipple. His fingers accelerated, pressing even more firmly.

"Henry!" she gasped, and he felt her clit grow harder and pulse underneath his fingertips as she cried out her orgasm.

He released her nipple and sank his fangs into her neck. She went limp in his arms. "Oh, fuck, Henry."

His fingers never stopped circling her clit, and she came again, hard and fast, as the aphrodisiac in his fang serum flowed through her veins.

Gripping his hair, she pulled him off her neck, taking his mouth with hers, tangling her tongue deep with his.

He purred against her lips. "Now, *mi amor*, what would you like to do?"

"You are the devil himself," she whispered back.

"There are times I agree with you."

"Sit. Drink. Give me a chance to catch my breath." She handed him the wineglass of alcohol-infused blood. He sat together with her and watched as she sipped from her own glass.

A few swallows of dark wine later, the alcohol hit his bloodstream, warming him all the way to his toes. The soft relaxation didn't dampen his arousal one iota. If anything, it loosened the desire in him.

He wanted her now.

To clear his palate, he took a mouthful from her wineglass and swished it around. Drinking a small amount would do no harm.

She accepted the wineglass from him and, after another sip, set it aside. Then, with a twinkle in her gaze, she untied his robe, acting as if she was opening another present. Eyeing his ribbon-wrapped *pene*, she clapped her hands together. "Is that for me?"

A deep laugh had him choking on the wine he'd just swallowed. "It is all for you."

Kneeling in front of him, she made a show of untying the bow, and her light touches drove him crazy as her breasts, cupped by the magenta bra, hung in full view. He groaned as desire shot through him, and his *cojones* tightened.

She lowered her mouth and kissed the tip, then opened wide to take him in.

"*Madre de Dios.*" He leaned back, bracing himself on his palms, and spread his legs wider, making plenty of room for her as she knelt forward. The sight of her gorgeous ass in the air almost unmanned him. Golden firelight glinted off one round cheek, and the magenta G-string wrapped her hips before the satiny material disappeared seductively between her thighs.

As much as he wanted to thread his fingers through her hair to hold her tight and guide her, he wanted her to set the pace, to let her please him without his guidance. He stayed braced with both hands on the floor behind him.

Despite prior accusations, he didn't need to be in control *all* the time.

When she lowered her mouth again, sucking and tonguing him sinfully, she took him all the way to the back of her throat and kept going.

"Oh, *si*," he said with a moan.

He didn't want her to stop. As much as he enjoyed plunging himself between her legs, sometimes the heightened sensation of her mouth pleasuring him was what he wanted. And she wasn't averse to giving it.

Fang serum still hummed through him from his earlier sips at her neck, and it didn't take long for Cerissa's expert attention to bring him to the edge, for him to feel that tingle at the base of his spine, to want to lose himself to her.

"Cerissa, *oh Dios mío*, Cerissa!"

She sank all the way down, taking all of him and sucking hard.

He exploded, jerking his hips as she swallowed around his *pene* and milked his erection dry, massaging him until she drank every drop. Then she continued to suck lightly as he softened.

When he shifted his weight off his hands and touched her shoulder, she rose, sitting back on her bottom, legs crossed, and reached for her wineglass. After a sip, a bead lingered on her lips, begging to be sucked off. Who was he to resist such gracious temptation? Laving her lips, he delved in sensuously when she parted with a moan tasting the sharp flavor of himself mixed with the wine's rich dark cherry and blackberry notes with a hint of spice.

When they broke from the kiss, he hugged her tightly to him. "Give me an hour, and we can do whatever you had originally planned."

She laughed. "The setting was my idea."

She stretched out on the nest she'd built, and he lay next to her. She ran a finger over his chest and abs, and his *pene* twitched in anticipation, growing hard again when she touched his shaft.

The minx. She'd used her aura.

"We can do whatever you want," she added.

Through the crystal, he could feel her wanting more, as if her touch hadn't been enough to communicate her request. "Then I guess I don't need that hour after all," he said.

Consumed by his love for her, he snapped the bra's hooks, slipping it off to leave her breasts bare, then lifted her hips to slide off the thong. He shrugged off his robe and rolled her over on her back, her legs spread, and, without taking a beat, slid into her with a moan. She was so wet. Pleasuring him had aroused her all over again.

He hovered over her, staring into her ardent emerald eyes and tangling his fingers through her thick, wavy hair as he supported himself on an elbow. "I love you."

"Love you too, Quique."

She'd raised her legs, wrapping them over his thighs, but he wanted her opened wider. Moving back, he hooked her knees with each arm, then lifted her enough so she could tuck a pillow under her bottom and rest her inner knees on his shoulders. He braced on his palms and moved his hips slowly, watching his *pene* pull out, then thrust back in to grind against her sensitive nub.

Her back arched, raising her breasts prominently. He wasn't done paying attention to those beauties, and leaned forward, capturing a nipple gently between his lips. He sucked, using his tongue to tease the tip.

"Oh my," she said, thrusting her hips in sync with his.

He loved how she let him lead, let him set the pace, let him go slow and easy until he was ready to push her over the cliff. Now that they'd slaked the initial desire driving them, he could take his time, and changed nipples, taunting the other one with luscious licks and gentle pulls as he continued to thrust, gliding in and out of her, rebuilding their passion.

Her moans told him he was right on target.

Something about the moment reminded him of the first time they'd made love. She'd been so excited that night, but also so nervous, and afraid of being judged. Now, he excited her, but she was comfortable sharing her body with him, and he'd never judge her. Never judge what she needed to orgasm, never judge what she enjoyed in bed.

He'd gladly give her anything she desired to be happy.

Releasing her nipple, he kept thrusting while he brushed the hair from her face and looked into her eyes, then devoured her mouth in a skin-searing kiss. He could stay like this forever, coupled to her, deep into her body, her heart, her soul.

She tightened around him. The sensation told him she was close to coming again, and he moved his hips faster, gliding over her clit with each thrust, giving a little grind at the end. Panting, she whispered his name, then, with a moan, arched her back, driving him deeper inside as she peaked.

The way her inner walls clenched his shaft sent him over the edge. His orgasm shot through him, and he held on tight to her as his own moan escaped against her neck.

When the erotic pulses ebbed, he rolled them on their sides, still connected, keeping them locked together.

A year ago, if anyone had told him about the joy to be had in finding the love of his life, the simple domesticity of making love in front of a fireplace, the companionship of a bright and loving woman, he would have dismissed the suggestion.

Now he knew the truth.

"Merry Christmas, Henry," she whispered.

"Merry Christmas, *mi amor.*"

CHAPTER 4
CONSEQUENCES

RANCHO BAUTISTA DEL MURCIÉLAGO—CHRISTMAS DAY LUNCH

At noon, Cerissa met Karen at the door and laughed. "I love the Christmas sweater."

Karen wore one of those silly holiday pullover sweaters, green with a big angel on it, and handed Cerissa a small ice cooler to carry. "One of my siblings sent it. Thought you might appreciate the image."

"It's perfect for our talk with Jayden." Cerissa had chosen jeans and a fancy blouse. Casual, but festive in its own way. She'd tucked a sarong in the downstairs bathroom near the kitchen so she could easily change and morph for her planned demonstration.

They took all the leftovers into the luxurious kitchen Henry had built, which still struck her as strange, because he didn't need to cook. A stovetop burner and a pot of water was all he needed to heat his beverage of choice. But he enjoyed cooking—it was one of his ways of showing love.

She and Karen chatted lightheartedly as they prepared lunch. Cerissa barely had the sliced ham and the pasta casserole in the oven before the doorbell rang.

"I'll answer it. Finish getting things ready."

Karen had been putting salad into individual bowls. She snickered and gave a mock salute with the serving spoon. "Aye-aye, captain."

Oops. In her nervousness, Cerissa had forgotten the magic word. "Please."

"No worries." The doorbell rang again. "Go answer it before Jayden breaks the bell."

Cerissa rushed to the front door and found Jayden wearing civvies and a pensive expression, a pie container in his hands.

"Hi. Can I take that for you?"

"Ah, sure."

He'd brought pie for dessert—his mother's chocolate pecan pie recipe, according to the text message he'd sent. When she grasped the container and their hands brushed, he flinched.

She blinked. Was he uncomfortable touching her?

"Ah, we're in the kitchen." She led the way, carefully keeping the pie level. She didn't want it to slide within the container and bang into the side, breaking the crust. "Is everything okay?"

He pursed his lips. "We'll talk."

Uh oh. That didn't sound good.

Cerissa breathed deeply to calm her rising pulse. Some discomfort after discovering her identity wasn't atypical. Just look at how long it took Rolf to come around. Her mind knew that, but unease burbled through her stomach, and she willed herself to squash the kernel of disappointment blooming.

Once their plates were filled, they sat at the square mahogany kitchen table. Cerissa had removed the leaves and pushed the ends together to form a more friendly, casual dining arrangement. It didn't work. An awkward silence descended, and Cerissa speared her first bite of ham, her thoughts wandering deeper into the realm of anxiety.

His earlier flinch still bothered her. Was he struggling to accept the existence of the Lux? Jayden lived with vampires. Why wouldn't he be willing to embrace one more species? It wasn't so different. Besides, Tig had said he'd accepted the truth—just that he was still processing everything. But then, why was discomfort wafting off him in tumultuous waves?

Cerissa ate three more mouthfuls without tasting the leftovers until she couldn't endure the silence anymore. "Tig said you had questions."

"Yeah." Jayden set down his fork and leaned back. "And this is the first one: how could you? I thought we were friends."

The bite of cheesy pasta she'd taken caught in her throat, and she coughed. "We *are* friends."

He glared at her. "Are we? Or is that just another lie?"

Oh, he was angry—significantly so. She raised her chin. "No, it's not a lie. Even friends don't tell each other *everything*. I bet you have secrets from me."

"Something this big? That you're an angel, or alien, or whatever? No, I don't have a secret close to that. I feel like I don't even know you."

Cerissa swept up her glass and gulped the wine, swallowing hard, her mind fragmented as guilt seeped through her. He was right. She had hidden things from him. Significant things.

Seeing Jayden's anger, feeling it directed at her, her first instinct was to accept the blame and apologize. Yet she had an obligation to safeguard herself and her people, didn't she? Everyone had the right to shield themselves from harm.

With that, her guilt fell apart, and anger broke through the cracks, heating her chest. Why should she apologize for protecting her own life-threatening secrets? Jayden didn't tell any outsider the truth of his life.

Why the double standard?

She cleared her throat and tempered her response. "You're living with vampires. Is your family clued in?"

"Of course not. But on this side of the wall, we don't keep secrets from each other. Not ones this explosive. You betrayed our trust. You lied every day as though it was nothing."

"By omission, yes, but not directly. No one asked if I was mortal."

"No, you just pretend to be one of us."

"But it's not all pretend. I'm kind of mortal. My father was. What you see is an expression of his genes."

"But that's not the full story, is it? I've been fed lies all my life. I expect it from the perps, from those who break the law, from those who twist reality to fit their warped views. I didn't expect it from you."

Hurt flashed through her at the accusatory tone, tightening her throat, making her voice sound like a croak. "Jayden, this isn't just some choice I made without any consideration. It was a mandate to protect my entire species. When you learned about vampires after you'd dated Tig for a while, is this how you reacted?"

"That was different."

"How?"

"I... She never directly lied to me."

"And I didn't either."

"You did—you must have."

"Then so must have Tig."

"She didn't."

Cerissa narrowed her eyes. *That* she didn't believe, having seen how far vampires would go to hide their secret. "Tig didn't pretend to be mortal? She didn't misrepresent why she was only available after dark?"

"No—" Then he looked a little chagrined, and some of the anger leaked away, softening his frown. "Maybe."

"There are some secrets we keep for a reason. We do it not just to protect ourselves, but to protect mortals from their worst natures. And you're acting as if I *enjoy* lying to everyone."

"Prove you don't, then. Be honest with our community."

"Wait." She sat there frozen, his words sinking in, her thoughts moving in slow motion. "Are you suggesting I tell the rest of the Hill what I am?"

"Yes."

"Jayden—"

"You say your situation is similar to vampires, right? Vampires trust us within these walls. Why shouldn't you? Why is your secret so different from theirs?"

Cerissa covered her mouth, shocked. The truth about the Lux wouldn't be divulged anytime soon, not in his lifetime. But vampires had long memories. How would they react when the world discovered they shared a planet with another species? Her contact lenses were recording the conversation—maybe she should flag this for Agathe's consideration. The head of the Lux must have anticipated how the vampires would eventually react before embedding Cerissa in the Hill community, right?

She shook her head, derailing that train of thought with another. Had Tig told him nothing of her conversation with Agathe? Of the reason for secrecy? Her silence about her true nature couldn't be helped. Jayden wasn't "processing" the truth—he'd built an ultimatum to demolish Cerissa's life.

"Jayden, there are those on the Hill who would force me to leave if we tell them. That's if they didn't try to kill me."

"Who would try to kill you?"

"A good number of those who attended last night's party, that's who."

"Nah, Tig won't let them. But you're right, they may kick you out—and you should have considered that before lying to us."

What the hell? Did he *want* her banned from the community?

"I realize you feel betrayed right now, but do you really believe that... Do you think ostracizing me is a fair exchange for my protecting myself and my entire species?"

Jayden's jaw tightened. "Look, if there's one thing I've learned as a police officer, it's that transparency builds trust. Maybe if you were transparent now, you could build that trust back with our community in time." He appeared uncomfortable, as if he didn't want to say the next part. "There'll be questions from the council about whether your past testimony on DNA can be trusted. Like it or not, you're a police consultant. The rule applies to you, too. Tig's authority—hell, the entire department's—will be scrutinized. The whole of our integrity will be questioned, because of your lie. Your lie, *and* Ari's lie. I want you to fix it. Be transparent now, maybe salvage something."

Oh. Cerissa leaned back in her chair, her mind running in circles.

Obviously, she'd hurt Jayden. But that wasn't just it. She'd threatened what was dearest to him, even inadvertently. And now he'd taken that hurt and that threat and turned it into a demand for transparency on the hope that it might stave off some of the damage he predicted. She understood that, but it wouldn't work the way he thought it would. Still, she had to own her part in this. Sometimes, people could tell you what was wrong, how they'd been hurt, but their idea of a fix might make your situation worse.

The weight of the realization wrapped around her. Would everyone on the Hill react this way? In the very beginning, she hadn't considered the impact of her lie. Initially, the Lux had uncovered the threat posed by the Vampire Dominance Movement, and the vampire communities needed help to stop them. She had to be within a community to do that, and she had to pretend to be something she wasn't. All she had cared about at first was stopping the VDM.

But then she'd fallen in love with Henry and grown to care about Sierra Escondida and all the friends she'd made within it—like Jayden and Tig.

She'd wanted to live in a place where people lived as long as she did, and she figured that while someone might detect and expose the Lux within the next hundred years as mortal tech advanced, it was something to deal with then. She'd failed to contemplate the consequences when that happened. Of how people might react to not just what she was, but how she'd been keeping her identity from them. Would they react the same as Jayden? Would they be ready to banish her from the community when the truth eventually came to light? Would they see her as a threat one way or another? Would being friends with her for a lifetime not make a difference?

She didn't know.

But what was she supposed to do now?

She glanced over at Karen, who'd been eating during the entire conversation. "Help?"

"You want my help?"

"Yes!"

"Okay, okay." Karen grinned. "She's under orders not to tell anyone. If she does, she could get in very serious trouble with her own people, not just ours. Tig negotiated with the Lux's top dog, forced them to face the truth, or they wouldn't have allowed her to even tell you."

Jayden shook his head, his lips firming into a flat line. "So?"

Karen tilted her head. "What do you mean, 'so'? The Lux could pluck Cerissa away from here forever if she messes with their rules. Not just from Sierra Escondida, from everything. She answers to them. Do you just ignore whatever Tig tells you when you're on duty?"

Jayden clenched his jaw and remained silent.

"How many times have you lied to protect the Hill, Jayden? If one of your friends outside of these walls learned about vampires, would you reveal the whole of vampire society to prove you were sorry? You couldn't—literally and figuratively. I get you're pissed, but what you want her to do isn't an actual option."

He crossed his arms and his jaw hardened.

Cerissa wasn't sure how to deal with this. Maybe they could pivot to safer ground for now. "Jayden, I thought you had questions about my, ah, differences from mortals."

"Tig explained those. I'm more interested in hearing how you plan to make this right."

So much for pivoting. "I can't tell everyone about the Lux."

"It's not everyone. We're a small town. We can keep it limited to those who live here."

"We don't have the blood bond ability vampires do to stop community mortals from gossiping about us to outsiders. The blowback if news spread among mortals would be too great. Every person who learns the Lux exist increases the danger for my people."

"What's the danger, exactly? You have tech and powers we don't."

"We don't want war. If word leaked, mortals might start a religious war, the size of which you can't imagine. They might assume we're a harbinger of Armageddon once they saw our true forms. And even if they don't raze the world, then mortals and vampires might hunt us, and we'd have to defend ourselves. That'd start a different kind of war, one we don't want to engage in."

Jayden nodded, but his expression remained reluctant. "That's what Tig said."

Cerissa wouldn't apologize for protecting her people. But she did want to apologize for hurting Jayden with her lie. "I'm sorry I had to keep it a secret from you. I am."

Jayden *tsked*, sounding like a teakettle letting off steam. "I need to know: did you ever use your aura on me?"

Cerissa sat back, surprised. "I don't think I have." She rubbed at her temples, straining to remember. "When I was in jail, I might have, but I don't believe I did. But it's not something that stands out in my mind. I don't tend to recall it."

"How does it feel?"

Karen jumped in. "Sudden relaxation. Like it's easier to go along with what she wants than to fight it."

"Shit." Jayden scrubbed a hand over his shaved head. "Can I ever trust my perceptions of you again?"

Cerissa winced, then sighed. She could understand his concern. No one wanted to be manipulated or controlled. "I don't often employ my aura. Mostly to calm someone who's upset or injured. I don't see a reason I'd ever use it on you, except if you were badly hurt, and I needed to quiet you to start treatment."

"Honestly?"

"Yes, honestly." She tried smiling at him.

Silence stretched for a moment, and then he said, "I'm not sure where I'm at with all this. I'm angry. I hate how you lied. I hate the trouble it might make, too. But if we're going to move forward from here, we can start with no more secrets. Full transparency between us, at least, even if you can't tell the community yet. And we go from there."

"I want to rebuild our trust, I do. So, I'm being honest now when I say this: I can only promise I'll do my best. The Lux are monitoring all kinds of threats against mortals. Right now, none of them involve vampires, and I'm not briefed on those issues until I need to know about them."

"But when you are—"

"I'll request permission to share with Tig. It's part of our deal with her."

"Okay." Jayden still looked skeptical.

"Would it help to see my native form? That's some honesty I can give you now."

His gaze swept the kitchen, a hint of fear in his eyes. "You can do that here?"

"It's just us. Let me duck into the bathroom. These clothes won't fit my Lux body."

Moments later, she returned as a blue-skinned, white-winged angel, and wore the sarong she'd prepared. She held a translator in her six-fingered hand. "Questions?"

"Shit."

Cerissa waited. Nearly everyone asked to touch her ivory feathers when they first viewed her native form, but he didn't.

"Your wings... They're bigger than I expected."

She whirled around and spread her feathers, almost knocking dishes off the kitchen island. Karen made a mad dash to save a casserole pan.

"The wingspan is wide because it has to be for a body my size. But our bones are hollow, similar to a bird's bones."

"Tig said you can shapeshift into other animals."

"Many others, but here's what I most commonly choose on the Hill." She handed the translator to Karen, untied the sarong at the neck, and morphed into a cougar before the dress fell to the ground.

Jayden jumped from his seat, defensively pivoting the chair between them.

"It's okay," Karen said with a giggle. "It's Cerissa."

The cat yawned, showing off her sharp teeth, then closed her mouth and twitched her whiskers. On all fours, she strolled around Jayden, head-bumping his leg to scent-mark him.

He kept absolutely still.

Sensing he'd had enough, she snagged the dress with her teeth, loped to the bathroom, nosed the door shut, morphed, and dressed.

"Questions?" she asked when she rejoined them.

Jayden shook his head. "No, but maybe later."

Karen's grin broadened. "Admit it. It's cool, isn't it?"

Jayden huffed. "Yeah, maybe a little."

"You'll get used to it. And you'll remember all the times Cerissa has helped us, too."

Jayden's face lost some of the anger, and he seemed more contemplative than furious. "We'll see."

Cerissa nearly sighed in relief. That was an inch of progress for now. She'd accept it.

"Let's have pie," she said, smiling. "Oh, and if you get any reports of a mountain lion in the foothills, call Henry first. Since it might be me."

CHAPTER 5

SURPRISE

RANCHO BAUTISTA DEL MURCIÉLAGO—CHRISTMAS NIGHT

Between hosting *la tamalada*, then Christmas Eve socializing at Rolf and Karen's, followed by quality time with Cerissa, Henry had ignored his email. Tonight, they'd agreed to work separately, spending the early evening to make headway on business correspondence neglected during their vacation. In a few hours, they'd take a break and watch Christmas movies together. Maybe she'd tell him what was bothering her then. Over dinner, she seemed nervous, but he hadn't pressured her to talk about it. Sometimes she needed space to identify her feelings.

He'd only cleared about half of his inbox between arriving home from New York and celebrating the holiday. He had a lot more to get through now. One message from Rolf reminded him to expect a visit later, and he marked it as read.

He groaned when he saw the sender on the next message in the queue. *Anne-Louise.* Perhaps it was nothing more than a Christmas greeting. But when it came to his maker, trust in her motives, no matter how benign they seemed, remained an issue for him.

Surprise ratcheted through him when a link to an invitation manifested on screen. He checked to make sure his antivirus software was up to date and then clicked on the link. If it was a phishing scam, the security program should protect him from a harmful website.

No on-screen alert appeared. Rather, a lovely lavender envelope materialized, and an animated invitation emerged, moving like a magic carpet.

Henry shot to his feet and opened the French doors that separated their offices. Cerissa was sitting on the couch, her laptop open to building plans for her biotech research campus. The facility was currently under construction.

"Cerissa, have you seen this?"

He'd launched a second copy of the invitation on his phone, and extended it for her to see.

"Oh, how lovely! Rick and Anne-Louise have set a date." Then confusion filled her eyes. "It's the end of next week. Don't they have to wait a year?"

"They have been dating for three years, so no, there is no waiting period under those circumstances for the Collective."

"Are we going? I could get some flight time. I almost have my written lessons completed—"

"We were just there. The fuel to fly to the East Coast is expensive."

She gave him a coy look. "I could flash us there."

"That will not work, and you know it. Let me consider the matter."

"All right. We can discuss the invitation later."

He took her comment as a polite dismissal and turned away. He had other correspondence to complete before movie time and couldn't allow Anne-Louise's issues to distract him.

"Ah, Henry?"

Coming to a halt, he answered her. "Yes?"

"Jayden's angry because I kept what I was a secret." She explained his concerns about trust and betrayal.

Henry sat on the office couch next to her and clasped her hand in his. "I can't say I'm surprised. The community will be upset when they learn about the Lux. And in particular, when they learn one has always been among them, well, we may have to depart for a while until things calm down."

"What? You never mentioned—"

"Why distress you prematurely? Over the next seventy years, you'll slowly age yourself, at which point we'd have to fake your death. I assumed we'd move away and start over."

"I don't want to be the reason you have to leave. This is your community."

He squeezed her hand. "Thank you, *cariña*. But it's nothing we need to decide now. That moment is a long way off in the future, and we'll deal with it then, all right?"

"Ah, but those vampires—the mean ones who I avoided at Rolf's house. When they discover what I am, they'll be furious. They'll hate me even more."

Pulling her into his arms, he held her tightly to him. "They don't matter. Your friends will stand by you. Trust me."

"Are you sure? Our friends might feel the same as Jayden does—"

"Stop. Jayden is angry right now. Give him time. It may change. If we have to, we'll meet with each one of your friends individually and explain it before they learn from another source. Now quit worrying about problems that aren't here yet. So much could happen in the next hundred years." He kissed the top of her head. "Understand?"

"But—"

"Cerissa," he said sternly.

"Yes, sir."

A smile quirked his lips. "I like the sound of that."

She playfully slapped his chest. "Stop that. I'll let it go for now. But we'll ultimately need a plan."

"Of course. And I know I said we'd spend the evening together, but I'm expecting guests soon, and wanted to talk with you about something before they arrive."

"What is it?" She closed the laptop and set it aside.

"Rolf has been complaining. He's of the opinion that you are spoiling Sang and Mort. He trained them to be watchdogs, not lapdogs."

"If he'd just show them some affection, they wouldn't be so starved for my attention."

"I'm aware, *mi amor*, that you have a soft spot for his dogs. They seem to have found a kindred spirit in you." Henry suspected the dogs recognized she was the cougar who occasionally ran in their woods. And that she may have indulged in playing doggie tag with them while in cougar form. "But I need to keep the peace with Rolf."

"Well, what do you suggest? They come running to greet me as soon as I'm near Rolf's property."

"Just don't bring them food and toys. Rolf has said that he will make sure they have treats and playthings, but he does not want them accustomed to receiving food from anyone other than him and Karen. It makes them bad guard dogs. Do you agree?"

"If he promises to give them plenty of treats and toys, then I will refrain from bringing any over to his house."

"I knew we could arrive at a compromise on this," Henry said, "because—"

The doorbell rang, interrupting him.

"Ah, yes. Come, let's get the door."

R olf stood on their front porch holding the cutest German shepherd puppy Cerissa had ever seen. They'd tied a red ribbon in an enormous bow around his harness for Christmas. It was absolutely adorable.

"Oh my word, he's darling. I didn't know you two were considering getting another dog."

"We aren't," Karen said, staring at Cerissa from over Rolf's shoulder, glee on her face.

"You aren't—" Cerissa squinted at them, puzzled. If the dog wasn't another companion for Mort and Sang, then who was he for? "Wait—Henry, is this..."

"Yes, Cerissa, he's for you."

Rolf rolled his eyes, adding to the smug look on his face, and shifted the puppy to one arm to wave at the ribbon. "I thought this big red nonsense on his harness would have made that clear."

She squealed. Actually squealed. Joy filled her as she reached for the puppy. *Her* puppy.

Rolf swung to the side, holding the dog away from her fingertips. "Has she agreed to the terms?"

"Terms?"

"Yes, Rolf, she has."

"Very well." He plopped the puppy into her arms. "Merry Christmas. Try not to spoil him too much. It's not healthy for the dog."

"Oh, he's wonderful." She hugged the puppy to her, and he rewarded her with a big lick. His fur was solid blond, with a black blaze on his forehead and covering his muzzle. "Where did you get him?"

"From Sang and Mort," Rolf replied.

"What?" Surprise and confusion ruffled through her.

Karen laughed. "They had puppies. He's one of the litter."

Cerissa's jaw dropped. "Why did you keep her pregnancy a secret?"

Karen maneuvered around Rolf and came into the house, carrying a basket of puppy stuff. "Simple. Henry bribed me."

During their trip to New York, Cerissa had visited a pet store to buy birdseed, and Henry had patiently tagged along. When she sighed and petted the puppies on display, he knew she was getting one, but he'd said nothing. No hint. No smirk. No mixed message about how puppies were so messy.

No, he'd just let her long for one, fully mindful her longing was being fulfilled soon.

The rat fink.

She hugged the puppy close, and he yipped and licked her face again.

"Cerissa, do not let him lick you."

Now that sounded like the Henry she knew and loved.

Karen put an arm around Cerissa's shoulders. "Ignore the two grumpy old men. Let's go into the drawing room and I'll tell you everything you need to know about puppies. Have you ever had one before?"

"No, he's my first. How old is he?"

"Almost twelve weeks." Karen unfolded a blue plastic-backed pad and spread it on the rug covering the drawing room's hardwood floor. "Sang had her puppies on October first, and we had the hardest time keeping it a secret from you."

"That's why you were taking them to the vet so frequently."

"Yep. I almost slipped one time."

"I wondered why Sang was never around when I came over the last few times."

"She was in the room off to the side of the garage with the puppies. She had six of them. And they are all promised already. Yours is the first."

"I'll have to bring him by to visit his mother."

"No," Rolf said abruptly. "Don't do that. It's not good for Sang. Once the puppy is gone, it is better that she not see it again or she'll start hunting for it."

"Oh, that's sad."

"Yes, but Rolf's right," Karen said. "Sang will be fine, and the puppy will do well with you. What are you going to call him?"

"I don't know. It's all so sudden. I'll have to ponder it a bit—a name's a big thing." Even though Cerissa believed in science rather than magic, the Law of Names claimed that figuring out something's true name gave you power over it. She pursed her lips. How did one go about discovering a puppy's true name? Maybe something similar to his parents' names? "What about Fang?"

Henry and Rolf groaned.

"Well, you named yours 'death' and 'blood.'"

"Try to bestow him with a more normal name, please," Henry said.

She still couldn't believe that Henry was casually discussing the naming of their dog, that he'd even conspired to get her a dog. He'd always said he didn't want a pet, and yet, for her, he'd changed his mind. She sent a burst of love through the crystal to him.

Getting onto the floor with the puppy, she rolled on her back and lifted him in the air over her. He barked a little puppy bark. "Then I'll just have to wait until he tells me his name," she said, cuddling him to her chest. "Henry, where will he sleep?"

"That is entirely your decision. He is your puppy—all yours. I will not be responsible for him."

"Don't worry," Karen said. "His training has already started. We'll get you all set up. I brought his special food, a water dish, and, as you can see, piddle pads. We even have a sleeping kennel in the back of the Escalade for you, along with a dog bed. Tomorrow, you and I can go into town to the local pet store and get whatever else you need for him. On the day after Christmas, they have everything on sale. Tonight I can go over potty-training basics. Speaking of which, we should cart him outside soon and find a grassy area that you want him to use."

"Okay." The puppy was teething on one of her fingers as she held him. "Will his ears stand straight on their own?"

The tips bent over, unlike his mother's, which stood tall.

"That's normal for a German shepherd puppy," Rolf said. "As he gets older, they'll straighten. And he will probably have a black saddle on his back identical to his mother, but it's too early to tell."

"Come on." Karen headed to the front door. "We should get moving before he has an accident."

Cerissa followed. They decided on the patch of grass at the vineyard's edge. Not too close to the house, but near enough it wasn't an inconvenience to bring him there.

"We've already started his training in the portable kennel," Karen said. "He's been sleeping in it with the door open for a few weeks already. It's his space. But if you close the door, give him a bowl of water inside and don't leave him in for over four hours. His puppy bladder can't last that long. Make sure he's gone outside first, too."

"How do you figure the timing?"

"Age in months plus one equals the number of hours."

Cerissa wasn't sure if she approved of that. "I can also install a portable fence for him, right? In the kitchen? So he has a bigger space to roam?"

"Sure. Set the kennel inside the area with the door open. That way, he can still sleep in it. Some dogs prefer to; others don't. Let him decide."

The little guy sniffed around before finding a place to do his business and then tried to dash off into the bushes. The leash stopped him, the long take-up reel reaching its limit, and he struggled, trying to wiggle loose from the harness.

"Bullheaded, I see," Cerissa said with a laugh.

"Mort was the same way at first. He'll settle down, don't worry." Karen clapped her hands together and said, "Come here." He came running to her, and she swept him into her arms. They strolled back to the house. "So, are you going skiing with us?"

"Skiing?"

"Yeah, Rolf was going to invite you two. We booked a three-bedroom condo in Snowstone. It was all they had available, so we thought you and Henry should join us and stay in the extra bedroom. The guys can share the third one to sleep in during the day."

"We just got back from New York. And we may have to return. Anne-Louise and Rick are getting married on the sixth of January."

"Gotcha. We're going too. Anne-Louise invited me and Rolf, since she stays in our guest house when she visits the Hill. We can ski and then fly the jet to New York."

"I'm not sure. Henry promised to work with me on our wedding plans as soon as the holiday was over. We haven't even set the date yet."

"Not to worry. You're talking to an expert event planner—who do you think organizes all the party events promoting Vasquez Müller Winery?"

"Yeah, well, you do."

"Exactamundo! And I can provide the perfect wedding planner app to guide us and get everything done. We can start entering all the stuff directly to the website during our ski trip. So now you have to come."

"Admittedly, it sounds great, but I wouldn't want to leave the puppy alone that long."

"Bring him with. Excellent experience for him at his age. And I'll help you watch and train him. We'll have a blast!"

Cerissa loved the idea. But would Henry? He'd been nervous about money, and a second vacation seemed like an extravagance they should skip. "Let's see what happens when Rolf extends the invitation."

"You'll leave it entirely up to Henry?"

She took the squirming puppy back from Karen. "He's been so sweet about getting me a dog. I don't want to push him for something else."

Karen laughed. "That's when you should push. When the dice are hot, keep rolling."

CHAPTER 6
BABYSITTING DUTIES

RANCHO BAUTISTA DEL MURCIÉLAGO—A FEW HOURS LATER

After Karen and Rolf left, Henry introduced Cerissa to some of his favorite Christmas movies as she played with the puppy, who fell asleep in her lap. Soft beige leather covered the oversized captain chairs—recliners, really—in the media room. He wasn't happy to see the animal on his furniture, but he didn't want to spoil her fun. When the last movie ended, Henry left her playing with the puppy again and returned to his desk to clear a few more items off his to-do list.

An hour later, a cougar came trotting into his office carrying the puppy, gently grasping the scruff of its neck between her teeth. The dog didn't seem to mind, peacefully letting her carry him around without squirming or yipping. Could all animals sense it was still Cerissa? Or had she given him an infusion of her aura? That could account for the reduced puppy energy, too.

The cougar hoisted the blond bundle onto his lap. "I suppose you want me to watch him while you go for a run?" he asked as he petted the puppy.

She meowed in response. Knowing her, she'd assumed it would be harder for him to argue when she was in cougar form.

"All right." He stroked the puppy again as its sharp teeth wrestled with one of his fingers. "But we will not make a habit of this, understood?"

Another guttural meow.

"And you're going to have to name him soon."

She pulled on his sleeve.

"And I suppose you want me to let you out?"

She didn't answer but loped to the hallway and down the stairs.

"We'll use the front door so Christine doesn't see you." He followed her, carrying the puppy.

As soon as Cerissa was gone, the puppy whined. "You miss her already?" The puppy yipped, then whined again. "You'll have to make do with me until she comes back."

The dog's reply was to lick Henry's face.

"No licking." He placed his hand over the puppy's muzzle. "You are as bad as your mistress."

Henry carried the puppy upstairs and retrieved the fluffy daybed from Cerissa's room. He positioned it in his office near his desk and put the puppy on it, and had returned to his computer, intending to work, when the puppy made a mad dash for the hallway.

"Just where do you think you're going?" He chased after the dog as it bounded down the stairs, hit the throw rug in the foyer, and went sliding across the tiles until he crashed into the door. The puppy immediately sprang to all fours and started barking.

"Do you need to go out, or do you just want to chase her?"

Recognizing he wouldn't get an answer, Henry found the leash on a foyer side table and led the puppy outdoors with a sigh.

How had he gone from a carefree bachelor to mated with a vampire child and a puppy in only eight months?

When they got to the grassy area, Henry gave the "potty" command that he'd heard Karen say. The puppy circled and sniffed and soon did his business. Then he began pulling at his leash.

A walk, as well?

This was not how Henry foresaw it when he agreed Karen could give Cerissa the puppy. But it was a pleasant Christmas night after all. He let the dog lead—straight to Rolf, who came from the opposite direction, hiking through the vineyard that connected their properties.

Rolf laughed. "Puppy-whipped already?"

Henry growled his anger over the slight. "What are you doing here?"

"Karen wants you two to join us on our ski trip. I thought it best to talk in person. Didn't Cerissa tell you? Karen mentioned it to her."

"No, she didn't."

Rolf explained the plan, including the trip to New York. "We've already paid for the condo. A three-bedroom was all they had left. Accommodations and the jet ride are my treat, and a night of helicopter skiing. I don't want to jump from a helicopter on my own, and it's too advanced for Karen. You'll arrange lodging at the Collective for all of us. Fair enough?"

Henry considered it and sighed. Even if he arranged the New York accommodations, it was not an even trade. He hated accepting gifts. They made him feel obligated, but as Father Matt counseled, letting go of that would make him a happier person.

"Things are quiet at the winery," Rolf added. "William has the fermenting process under control. Come on, make the women happy. Cerissa told Karen she wanted to go but would let you decide."

Rolf was right. The assistant winemaker had everything well in hand. Henry glanced at the puppy on the leash. He did have a weakness for making his mate happy.

"Thank you. We accept."

After the puppy exhausted himself, Rolf left, and Henry returned to the house, settling the small bundle of energy onto the daybed with a squeaky toy. Soon, he heard a sharp *clang*, the metal pail on the front porch tipping over. That was Cerissa's signal to him she was back and wanted to come inside. The puppy made a repeat of the same antics, running down the stairs and sliding across the throw rug. Henry swept up the rug—he'd put it into storage for now. Holding the puppy by the harness to restrain his enthusiasm, he cracked the door for Cerissa.

Still in cougar form, she slunk in, nosed his fingers aside, grasped the puppy by the harness, and carried him into the drawing room. Henry shrugged and returned to his office. If he was going to be gone for another week, he had some work to take care of, even if it was still Christmas night.

When he heard something go crash in the drawing room, he was out of his chair and down the stairs at lightning speed. But all was well. Apparently, one of the end tables had toppled over when their game of chase escalated. Nothing broken. He righted the table and watched as the puppy continued to pursue Cerissa around the room.

Her cougar would dodge one way, then another, and the puppy tried to match her agility. When she pivoted to chase him, the puppy play-bowed and charged. Henry could feel Cerissa's delight through the crystal.

He considered cautioning her to be more careful, but then he thought better of it. If anything broke, he could readily replace it. He'd rather she was happy.

A moment of pride washed through him at the realization. He'd worked hard on his emotional growth and didn't have to control everything. Watching the two of them pursue each other for another few minutes entertained him, and then Cerissa plopped onto the rug, tired of the game. The puppy wasn't to be deterred so easily. He charged and tackled her back, rolling them both over. Bolting upright with puppy nimbleness, he jumped on her again, nipping at her ear.

Cerissa hissed at the pain, scrambled onto all four paws, and threw him off. But the puppy rushed her again. This time, she grabbed him by the scruff of his neck and trotted upstairs.

Henry chuckled as he followed the two of them. "Someone is in trouble."

Once in her bedroom, Cerissa nudged the puppy into his kennel, which contained his nighttime bed, then shut the door with her nose. She morphed back into human form.

"Ow," she said, rubbing her ear. "That little monster has teeth."

Henry examined her ear—the skin had healed instantly when she morphed, but a ghost of the pain must have remained. He kissed the shell, slipped his arms around her naked waist, then turned her to face him so he could play with one nipple. With a deep moan, she raised her chin and pressed her soft lips to his.

The puppy whined. She broke from the kiss and bent over, looking into the crate. "It's okay, baby," she said. "It's time for you to settle for the night."

The puppy continued to whine.

"Have you named him yet?"

"I wanted to get to know him first. But my first impression remains. He's curious, persistent, and demanding, just like those grizzlies in Yellowstone Park. So, I'm naming him Bear."

Henry laughed. "An apt name. But I believe part of the problem is you. You are spoiling him, just as Rolf warned you would. And I will not have Bear interfering with our love life."

Henry lifted the kennel. The puppy's weight made the boxy crate unbalanced, but in his hands, it was featherlight. He didn't wait for Cerissa to argue against moving Bear downstairs.

She grabbed a robe, tying the belt as she scurried to join him on the staircase. "Where are you taking him?"

"He can sleep in the kitchen for now."

She looked at him, aghast. "But he'll be all alone."

He tutted at her. "You are going to make a terrible mother someday."

"That's an awful thing to say, Henry Bautista. You take that back."

"Bear needs to learn how to be alone. And you need to learn how to let him."

He set the crate on the kitchen floor, rifled through the puppy food containers in the basket on the counter, and found what he wanted.

Kneeling, he said, "Stay," and fed the puppy a treat through the grate, then stood.

Henry put an arm around Cerissa. "Now, we can use this time to enjoy each other, or you can be angry with me. Which will it be?"

"You have an infuriating way of arguing sometimes. Do you know that?"

"Yes." He hugged and kissed her. "It's good for you."

She melted against him. "Well, Karen said he needed water if we were going to close him in there. Has he peed recently?"

"Shortly before you returned."

She tilted her head from side to side as if debating with herself. "I'll take him again later."

She filled his water bowl and quickly slipped it into the crate, distracting him with another treat. Finished, she placed a light kiss on Henry's cheek. "All yours."

"Indeed."

He led her upstairs and into her bedroom, where he untied her robe, slid his hands over her naked body, and covered her lips with his.

An hour later, he held her as she closed her eyes. Once he was certain she was asleep, he returned to his office. He had some minor matters to resolve, which had gotten interrupted earlier by the sound of a table crashing over.

As sunrise approached, he went to check on Cerissa. The puppy was cuddled in her arms, and both were sleeping soundly. She must have snuck downstairs to let Bear out, perhaps given him an early-morning feeding, and brought him to bed with her. She looked so peaceful, so beautiful, with the puppy in her arms.

Henry sighed, opening his heart to embrace them both. In a hundred years, she'd have children. And watching her with the puppy had given him an inkling of what kind of mother she'd be.

A very loving, caring mother. A little indulgent, but a very good one, indeed.

CHAPTER 7

FLIGHT CHECK

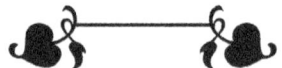

Standing on the airport tarmac, Henry handed the next bag to Rolf, who stood under the airplane with his head disappearing into the hold. He was determining how to stack everything so all the odd-shaped luggage would fit, including two pairs of skis.

Henry hadn't brought his, and Cerissa didn't own any. The last time he'd gone off-trail skiing, dropping from an open helicopter door into the back country, his bindings broke during an imprudent jump over a small ravine near the mountain's base, and he hadn't yet replaced them. He and Cerissa would rent for now. If they skied more often, they'd buy their own equipment then.

During the flight, he planned to allow her to take the controls. He explained his intentions to Rolf, who'd been arguing with him about it for the past ten minutes.

Right now, Henry wasn't sure who irritated him the most: Rolf, who wouldn't quit mouthing off, or his maker, who'd started tugging a few days ago on the bond between them for no apparent reason.

Rolf shook his head as he packed the next bag into the Dassault Falcon's hold. "I have two words to describe that proposal, Henry—not good."

At least his friend hadn't called him pussy-whipped, which he'd done on prior occasions. The insult alluded to both Cerissa becoming a cougar—a pussycat—and the other, cruder meaning.

"Why do you think it's a poor plan?" Henry asked. "She's smart. She's been reading the training manual and her test scores are perfect. Why not instruct her and allow her to log hours?"

Rolf scowled. "It's not her ability I doubt. It's the wisdom of trying to teach or supervise your mate in anything. An entirely bad idea."

"Karen works for the winery you and I own."

"We're the exception to the rule. Besides, she reports to you. We set it up that way on purpose, remember?"

Point made. Henry had agreed to the change in the organizational structure to accommodate Rolf and Karen's relationship. "Cerissa is not like most mortal mates. I don't see the problem."

"It's your funeral." Rolf shoved in another bag and wiggled things around to make them all fit.

"One of our mates should learn how to pilot. If we get caught in a situation where we cannot land, and sunrise is approaching, Cerissa could get us to safety."

"Yes, I approve of the idea in general. But I don't care if she is an alien, or angel, or whatever. You should have a stranger teach her. Anyone but you."

"We discussed it. That would be a complete waste of money. I'm a certified flight instructor. She's done the basic work."

Henry enjoyed teaching other vampires how to fly. With a vampire instructor, no one questioned why the course occurred at night, and he charged a premium for his services—Señor Bautista knew the worth of his time.

"Mark my words, Henry. You may know how to teach someone to fly an airplane, but you should not try it with your mate."

"I said I would instruct her so she could log her hours, and I will." They'd also discussed having Ari supervise her flight time, to which Cerissa had responded with a fiery "no way." It had warmed him to hear she trusted him over Ari as an instructor. "This will be very easy."

Rolf laughed. "I would place a wager on that, but I don't feel like taking your money when there's no sport in it."

Irritation rumbled through Henry. He didn't have money to waste on a bet. Finances continued to be tight for him. Yet he wanted to bet his friend, badly, so he could *win* and experience the exhilaration that came with it. The excitement knocked aside certain annoyances currently clawing at him. "You refuse to bet because you have no confidence in your position."

There would be no problem with the flight lesson. In the cockpit, the roles were clearly delineated. Henry was the pilot, and Cerissa was the student. He was in charge, and she would follow his directions. But in other things? It was different when it came to planning the wedding, which he'd been putting off. With the wedding they were equals and would have to work through what each desired. With Anne-Louise's tug on the maker-child bond bothering him as well, he wasn't sure he could peacefully discuss some of the contentious issues wedding planning might raise...which was why he kept putting it off. Maybe after the trip to NY finished, they could start.

"You'll see." Rolf lifted the last suitcase that would fit, slid it in, and shut the hatch to the luggage compartment, before turning the handle and locking it. "Go through with this and you'll feel the sting of it without the added humiliation of paying me." With a carry-on bag in each hand, Rolf skipped jauntily up the seven-step stairs built into the jet's dropdown door, shooting a cocky smile over his shoulder.

Henry contemplated a witty riposte but didn't say it soon enough. The other SUV arrived, with Karen at the wheel and Cerissa in the passenger's seat. They parked in the hangar next to Rolf's SUV, then emerged and headed toward him.

He bowed. "Ladies."

Cerissa gave him a quick kiss. "Sorry about the delay, Henry."

"It's my fault." Karen clicked the SUV's key, and it beeped. "I forgot something at the winery and had to go back for it."

The rear compartment hatch rose, and Henry strode to the SUV. Bear yipped at him from his travel carrier. Next to the puppy sat four full cartons. Each contained twelve bottles of his specially blended reserve wine, their most expensive offering.

He stared at the corrugated cardboard boxes, the contents worth almost five thousand dollars in total and groaned. Right now, he couldn't compete with the way Rolf and Karen spent money. "Why do you need all that?"

Karen crossed her arms and spoke in her marketing voice. "Two cases are a gift to Anne-Louise and Rick for their wedding reception. Plus, we're on vacation. Cerissa and I will enjoy a few bottles, and we might visit the local wine shops, distribute samples, encourage them to carry our winery's catalogue. Then we can write off the entire trip as a tax deduction."

Henry snorted his disbelief. "The cost of that wine is more than the tax benefit."

Rolf joined them in the hangar and slapped Henry's shoulder. "You have to spend money to make money. Who taught me that?"

Cerissa laid her hand on his arm. "I'm sorry. It's partially my fault. We needed a wedding gift. Anne-Louise asked for the reserve wine, and I told her she could count on it for the reception."

Was this why his maker was tugging on the bond? To ensure the wine came with them? He growled underneath his breath. "She couldn't make do with our award-winning Cabernet?"

"I should have checked with you first, I know. But she asked, and I felt too embarrassed to say I had to get your permission. I was going to pay for it from my savings." She tilted her head, and her eyes pleaded, much like Bear did when he wanted something. There was no resisting Cerissa when she looked at him that way.

Henry ground his teeth. He'd compensate for the lost revenue somehow. "Rolf and I will share the expense."

He refused to make a profit directly off his mate. Even if she offered only the base cost of the goods, his pride wouldn't let her pay *his* winery for the gift.

Madre de Dios, he hadn't come to the point financially where he couldn't give his mate his own wine. "The cartons may come." He lifted Bear's travel kennel out of the trunk. "This is all your fault," he said to the puppy as he carried the crate up the stairs into the plane.

Rolf followed with two cases of wine, mumbling, "Puppy-whipped."

Cerissa opened the backseat door and grabbed her carry-on bag, then felt Karen's arm slink around her shoulders.

"I told you so," her friend whispered, laughing.

Cerissa frowned. "It feels so manipulative. I should have asked him first. I could still pay for it—"

"Don't worry about it. He enjoys spoiling you."

"If you say so."

"Absolutely. Trust me on this."

Was it smart to accept relationship lessons from Karen? Cerissa threw the strap of a large, rectangular bag over her shoulder and climbed the short staircase into the plane. The bag contained Bear's stuff, and she clutched her smaller carry-on in one hand. The two Cadillac SUVs would stay in the hangar while they were gone.

Rolf pushed past them to load the rest of the wine. Cerissa crossed through the narrow galley into the passenger area and dropped the last of her bags next to Bear's travel carrier. When the puppy saw her, he yipped and whined.

"Cerissa, please join me in the cockpit for the preflight check," Henry said, leading the way forward.

Rolf focused on her, a sly grin on his face as he hummed a funeral march.

She eyed him quizzically, her brow scrunched. *What the heck?*

Before Henry disappeared into the cockpit, she asked, "Shouldn't I stay with Bear?"

Karen waved them on. "Rolf will watch the puppy. He'll be fine."

Squeezing past Henry in the galley, Cerissa headed to the pilot's seat and whispered, "Rolf is being weird."

Henry kissed her as she passed by, pressing his body against hers—more so than required by the narrow space. "Ignore him."

She quirked her lips and confirmed the door with the built-in stairs was shut and secured. She then eased onto the pilot's chair, and he slipped into the copilot seat.

Karen followed and leaned against the bulkhead between the galley and the cockpit.

"And just where are you going?" Rolf gripped Karen's arms and held her back.

"I thought I'd sit in the jump seat and watch. Might learn something."

Cerissa glanced over her shoulder as Rolf directed Karen back to the cabin. "If you want to learn to fly jets, *Liebling*, you can take lessons during the day. Leave Henry to his own funeral."

Cerissa could hear their conversation even though a divider wall and short galley separated the pilot compartment from the passenger area. As she went through the preflight checklist, she took occasional glimpses through the doorway opening to see what was happening.

"I don't understand," Karen said. "He's giving her a lesson, so I might as well piggyback."

"I don't think this lesson will last very long. And you don't need to be there when the fight starts."

Fight?

Cerissa finished the checklist as she considered his words. Then it hit her.

He believes we can't work together.

She huffed, resolved to play nice with Henry and prove Rolf wrong.

"But I was—" Karen began.

"You'll still do what I say. Stay here in the cabin with me." Their conversation paused, and Cerissa could swear she heard kissing sounds. "Besides, if the lesson goes well, you and I can use the bedroom. It's about time we join the mile-high club."

Cerissa suppressed a giggle.

"Rolf, you're incorrigible," Karen said. "We can't go back there; we have to watch the puppy."

Enough was enough. Cerissa grasped the pilot's handheld microphone and flipped it to intercom. Suddenly, the loudspeaker in the plane came to life. "This is your pilot. Prepare for takeoff. Buckle your seatbelts."

"Let me go," Karen squealed.

"I can be your seatbelt."

Cerissa heard light slapping and looked through the open doorway. Karen batted at Rolf's arms, which were fastened firmly around Karen's waist, holding her in his lap in one of the oversized lounge chairs.

She keyed the microphone again. "Everyone in their own seats, please."

Karen laughed. "With Captain Cerissa at the controls for the first time, I'd better buckle up."

CHAPTER 8

CLEAR SKIES

Henry ignored Karen and Rolf's flirting. Cerissa's lesson was proceeding fine so far, Rolf's caution notwithstanding. The preflight check went well—Cerissa hadn't missed a thing, and she was ready to taxi toward the runway. She called the tower and received clearance to bring the plane into position.

During their previous flights to and from New York, he hadn't let her command the plane. Especially on the return flight after she'd drunk a martini with dinner. Since then, she'd completed all her written and simulator tests. A shorter hop to Colorado was the perfect opportunity for her to get some actual pilot time.

"Go easy on the power until we're on the runway," Henry said.

"Got it. I read the manual." She sounded preoccupied as she handled the controls and steered toward the takeoff lane. When she reached the starting line, she radioed the tower. "Ready for departure."

"Cleared for takeoff," the air traffic controller replied. "Have a good flight."

"This is a short runway," Henry said. "You need to achieve lift speed quickly."

"Yes, Henry." She raised the throttle, sending power to the engines, and began building speed for liftoff.

He braced himself. "Not too quickly."

"Yes, Henry."

Was she listening to him? She accelerated along the runway rather fast for a beginner. Beginners tended to be more timid, more cautious. The amount of thrust she applied wasn't typical for her. When she drove a car, she didn't exceed the speed limit. But now, she goosed the power then pulled back on the yoke to get lift, and Henry felt the wheels leave the ground. She gunned it again and rapidly climbed.

He hovered his hand over the control switch. If she got into trouble, he could flip the switch and assume command. "Easy, Cerissa—we have passengers. The idea is to gain altitude but not rocket straight up."

"Nothing wrong with my acceleration. Since there are homes below us, the regulations require us to gain cruising altitude quickly. We'll level out in thirty seconds and counting."

"This is not a space shuttle. You do not have to go so fast to gain altitude. Ease off and level."

"Twenty-three seconds to go."

He growled. "No. Now."

"But Henry—"

"Or I will take over the controls."

"Fine." She backed off on the flight speed and leveled out. "Why are you so irritable?"

He ignored her comment. "All right, you are at fifteen hundred feet. Now bring us up to ten thousand, but more slowly this time. It should take you at least twenty minutes to gain that altitude. Do you understand?"

"Yes, sir."

The tone made her opinion unmistakable, and he ignored it. "Now set course for Colorado."

She banked the plane and took the planned heading. It was a clear night, with few clouds.

"Very nice. That was better."

"Henry, I've flown before. What's going on?"

He glowered at her. "You have flown with wings. But have you ever flown this class of jet before?"

"Not this large, but Ari let me fly a small Cessna."

So she'd already worked with her cousin before and her earlier "no way" came from experience. No wonder she ratcheted the Falcon into the air so fast if Ari had been her first tutor. "There are major differences between being at the wheel of a propeller-powered plane for a short period and piloting a medium-sized business jet. So you'll listen closely to my instructions, and you'll follow them, or you can go sit in the cabin with Karen, and Rolf and I will take turns at the controls."

"You don't have to give me an ultimatum."

"I'm giving you instructions."

"No, you're being unnecessarily bossy about it."

He felt his temper flare as the jet slowly gained elevation. "Rolf was right."

She narrowed her eyes at him. "When is Rolf ever right?"

"I should not try to teach you to fly. I should hire an instructor and let them teach you. You will be more respectful to a stranger than to me."

"That works both ways, Henry."

He growled deep in his throat. "I have been completely respectful."

An alarm sounded. While he'd argued with her, they'd approached the first mountain range without gaining sufficient altitude.

"Increase your airspeed and pull up."

She followed those instructions immediately.

Rolf stuck his head in the cockpit. He was shirtless. "Is everything okay?"

"It'll be fine," Henry replied. "Just a minor glitch."

She sniggered. "He hasn't started yelling at me in Spanish yet, so all is well."

"We are barely five minutes out of the airport and you've already had an altitude alarm," Rolf said brusquely. "That shouldn't have happened."

Henry didn't need any help. "Nothing went wrong. Go back to the cabin."

Rolf seemed to consider something, then he pivoted and disappeared. He returned a moment later, wearing a shirt.

"I can't relax knowing she is flying. I might as well grab the copilot seat."

Henry raised an eyebrow. "*You* will teach her?"

"I'll do a better job than you will. Go on, get up."

Henry started mumbling in Spanish but switched the plane to autopilot and surrendered the instructor controls. Rolf was right. He wasn't doing his best job.

But being mated to Cerissa was only part of the reason he lost his temper and his focus. There was an additional excuse for his edginess, an unseen tug at his chest, a command to obey, and it wasn't coming from his fiancée.

No, the annoying call came through the blood bond with Anne-Louise, a bond that wasn't dying fast enough despite his maker's promise to let him go. The call demanded his attention, adding to his growing irritation, and vexed him until he was at the end of his patience with everyone.

And it had shown during his attempt to teach Cerissa.

Rolf commandeered the copilot's seat. "Now, knock off the attitude," he said to Cerissa. "Once you get your pilot's license, you can have all the attitude you want. Until then, you have no status on this plane. And I'm not Henry. You will not argue with me, or I will take over the controls and you won't pilot for the rest of the trip, *verstehen Sie mich*?"

"Yes, I understand."

"Good." Rolf settled in and glanced over the panel gauges. "Now, I want you to switch off the autopilot and fly manually. You might as well get familiar with the feel of the jet."

Figuring Rolf had things under control, Henry left the cockpit and relaxed onto a seat in the passenger area. In the chair across from him, Karen read a book and sipped a glass of wine, a silly grin on her face.

How had he let himself get kicked out of his own cockpit? Bear looked at him from his travel carrier and whined.

"I know how you feel, boy."

Henry opened the kennel door and let him loose. The puppy was so happy to be free, he ran around the cabin sniffing every piece of furniture, wagging his tail furiously.

While keeping a close watch on Bear to ensure the dog didn't lift its leg on the leather seats, Henry unzipped the portable bed. He found one of the pup's stuffies and lured him over.

"Okay, settle down." He stroked the puppy. "At least one of us needs to stay out of the doghouse."

Cerissa hated that Rolf had been right, and was angry with herself for letting Henry's need to control every little detail get to her. She didn't want to admit the truth: she was just as happy to have Rolf as an instructor. He continued giving directions, keeping her busy with lesson after lesson—going from manual to automatic and back again; changing altitude smoothly; anticipating changes in weather and how that would affect their flight path.

After she mastered those lessons, he peppered her with questions, what to do in this emergency or that. He kept her busy and focused, and by the time two hours had gone by, she was ready to relinquish the controls to the next pilot. Fatigue sank deep into her bones.

"Henry, please come to the cockpit," Cerissa announced over the loudspeaker.

He stuck his head in. "What, no blood on the floor?"

"Hilarious," she said with an eye roll thrown in. "Show a little respect."

"Of course, *mi amor.*"

"I'm ready to yield the seat for now. I'm tired. Do you want to take over the pilot's chair?"

"Certainly, *cariña.*"

"Rolf, you have the controls," she said.

Rolf nodded briskly. "Roger that."

The tiny space was too small for two adults to swap seats simultaneously, and Rolf would fly in the meantime. She unbuckled the seatbelt. "Thank you, captain."

Rolf kept his gaze directed out the cockpit's window. "You're welcome."

She wedged herself sideways to let Henry pass in the galley, then watched as he smoothly slid in to replace her. He checked the controls and gave Rolf side-eye. "Do not say it."

"I'm glad I didn't take your money on the bet, but you owe me for the two-hour lesson. I expect to be paid the going rate."

She didn't ask what the bet was about—she could guess easily enough—and left the galley. Once in the cabin, she collapsed onto the nearest comfortable chair.

Bear was asleep at Karen's feet. "How'd it go?"

"How do you think? A bit rough, at first. But Rolf is a decent instructor."

"Henry was in a snit, but he got over it."

"Good. He's not very patient. I'm glad Rolf intervened."

Karen stuck out her tongue. "I'm not. We were going to get some sack time, but Rolf couldn't focus after he heard the alarm."

"Sorry about that. Henry and I were arguing, and I wasn't watching the controls. Did you pack any food?"

"Check the refrigerator. I put a light supper in there—all cold foods. I didn't feel like making anything fancy."

Cerissa rummaged through the choices, found cheeses and sliced deli meat, and made a sandwich. That would keep her until they landed at Eagle County Regional Airport in Colorado.

About twenty minutes later, Rolf's voice came over the intercom. "Cerissa, please come to the cockpit."

She looked at Karen and raised both brows.

"Don't ask me," Karen said.

Cerissa rose and went forward through the narrow galley. She stuck her head in the cockpit. "Yes?"

"You'll take the copilot's chair. Watch Henry—he's an excellent pilot. But do not annoy him. He needs to stay focused on keeping us in the air."

"Sure. Let me check on Bear first."

She reentered the cabin and gently scooped up the sleeping puppy, placing him in his carrier. He rolled over, made a small snore, and continued snoozing. Then she returned to the cockpit.

Rolf placed his hand on Henry's shoulder. "Will you be okay?"

"I'm fine. Go back and enjoy yourself."

Rolf slid past Cerissa, and she got into the copilot seat.

After a moment, Henry said, "I should not have tried to teach you. It was my mistake for trying."

"I could have made it easier for you, too."

"Perhaps, but I believe Rolf is right. Mates aren't meant to be teacher and student. We'll hire an instructor, and you'll finish your coursework with them. Agreed?"

"Agreed." She leaned over and kissed him on the cheek. He took her hand and raised it to his lips, showing a little fang as he eyed her seductively. It felt nice to see he was interested.

She peeked back into the cabin. Karen and Rolf were gone—most likely to the small bedroom at the back of the plane. Why did that make her feel a little uncomfortable? Hopefully, they wouldn't be noisy.

"Do not worry—the bedroom is soundproofed."

Her eyes widened. "How did you know what I was thinking?"

"It was more what you were feeling. A strong feeling of discomfort coupled with embarrassment. I guessed Karen told you of their plan."

"She mentioned it."

"Perhaps they will do the same favor for us on the flight to New York. There is no reason both Rolf and I need to be in the cockpit for the entire trip." He tilted his head and flashed a little more fang.

She warmed inside and smiled a lopsided grin. "It's good to know our fight didn't dampen your appetite."

"*Cariña*, I love you. Nothing dampens my appetite for you."

"Same here." She locked gazes with him. "I love you too, Henry."

A leer appeared on his face. "Even if we will not have an opportunity on the plane tonight, the evening is still young."

The past few nights had been hectic as they got ready for the trip, leaving them with no time for lovemaking. She grinned back at him. "It is. It certainly is."

CHAPTER 9
HAPPY LANDINGS

COLORADO AIRSPACE—TWENTY MINUTES LATER

Henry reached for the microphone switch to announce preparations for landing, and Cerissa's hand stopped him. "What if they're still in bed?"

"Then they must get out of bed. Rolf can't claim ignorance of how much flight time we had left. If he hasn't finished by now, it's his own fault."

He flipped the microphone switch and announced they were starting their descent shortly.

A few minutes later, Rolf poked his head into the cockpit and gripped Henry's shoulder. "Conditions outside look decent for landing. You don't need me in the copilot's seat." Then he turned to Cerissa. "Watch what Henry does. Touching down on a frozen tarmac is difficult. He's excellent at it. You might learn something."

Rolf swung around and exited the cockpit.

Getting clearance from the control tower, Henry started the approach. Peace filled him at the sight of pine-covered mountains capped in deep snow. As he'd never lived in ski country, the visual cues accompanying their arrival signaled *vacation starts now* in his mind.

If only Anne-Louise would stop tugging on the bond. They were bringing the wine. What more could she want?

With mild crosswinds and an icy runway presenting the only obstacles, Henry safely landed the plane at the small regional airport. He taxied to a hangar provided by Airco Services. There, the Falcon would stay protected from the snow and sleet and receive a thorough mechanical check before they flew off again in five nights.

Once parked, Henry handed out their heavy coats from the tiny closet behind the cockpit, and Cerissa put little boots on Bear to protect his paws from the frozen tarmac. The puppy didn't take long to find a spot to pee so Cerissa could load him into his travel carrier again. The rental car company had delivered an SUV as requested. Big enough for the four of them, and their gear and luggage, including all the stuff traveling with a puppy entailed.

The formal outfits they'd wear to the wedding in New York remained in separate garment bags on the plane, hung in the small coat closet.

The drive to Snowstone—a mountain renowned for its premier night skiing—took less than an hour. Henry had introduced Rolf to the joys of skiing the ungroomed, rough terrain of back country over twenty years ago. Now Rolf frequented the slopes more often than Henry did. But he was back. Excitement revved through his veins. The thrill of returning to the double black diamond runs and anticipating the helicopter drop put him in a better mood.

The condo at Mountain Tops resort came with a covered parking space. After stamping his feet to dislodge the slush from his boots, Henry carried in the last of the luggage.

"Everything is inside," he said. "Let's unpack."

"Ow," Cerissa yelped.

Henry's eyes jerked in her direction as she dropped one of Bear's playthings—a tug-of-war rope.

"What happened?"

"This little beast cinched up on the rope and clipped me with his teeth. They're as sharp as a shark's."

She stuck the bleeding finger in her mouth.

"That is my job." A flap of skin oozed blood. Henry lifted her hand and licked the wound, feeling slightly guilty over enjoying the rich taste when she was in pain. "You'll have to teach him restraint."

"No kidding."

Henry licked one more time, savoring the flavor. "There." He released her hand. "The bleeding has stopped. Do you want to heal it?"

"I should"—she scowled at the puppy—"because blood attracts sharks."

The puppy yipped and dragged the knotted rope over to her feet, where he dropped it.

"You think I'm giving you a second chance tonight?" Cerissa stood, scooping Bear into her arms. The tug-of-war toy dangled from his mouth. "Which room is ours?"

Henry gestured to the door to the left of the living room. "They are both master bedrooms with en suite bathrooms. We have this one."

Rolf and Karen would have the one on the other side. Now that they each had mates, Henry preferred the separation, not wanting to share a wall through which sounds might penetrate.

Cerissa followed him. He stopped her. "Bear will sleep in the kennel in the kitchen."

"He's wide awake." She resumed walking into the bedroom. "Why are there bunk beds in the third room?"

"Apparently, the owner expects to rent this condo to families with children."

"It just seems strange for full-grown men to sleep in children's bunk beds with SpongeBob comforters."

He wouldn't let her get his goat. "It does not bother me. We'll mask off the window so no sunlight penetrates. We've done this before."

"As long as it works for you two. Let's unpack. I want to find our swimsuits." She placed the puppy on his daybed, gave him another chew toy, and said the "stay" command. "Karen and I plan on using the hot tub. The patio is enclosed."

Henry eyed Bear, suspecting he'd be off the bed as soon as Cerissa left the room.

"Here." She handed him a pair of swim trunks.

"I forgot to mention that Rolf and I usually don't bother—"

"Get that idea out of your head. I'm not getting into the spa naked with our friends."

He lifted his hands in surrender, changed, and left Cerissa alone to braid her hair. In the living room, he found Rolf unpacking the video game console.

Rolf raised his brows. "Clothing in the hot tub?"

"Humor her, please?" Henry shared his friend's more European, easygoing attitude about nudity and found nothing wrong or sexually inappropriate in hot-tubbing nude. But he'd accommodate Cerissa's preferences. "I'm sure Karen packed a pair of trunks for you, as she and Cerissa would have discussed this in advance."

"Bah," Rolf scoffed. "Sexually uptight angels. First the fight on the plane, and now this. Is Cerissa in charge, or are you?"

"Cerissa and I are still adjusting to being a couple. I appreciated your help with her flying lesson, and I will pay you for your trouble. But there were benefits there for you, too—such as your activities with Karen in the back of the plane."

Rolf's lips quirked up, which came off as a leer. "I'll concede Karen and I had fun. But that thing you call your fiancée isn't dictating the rules for our entire trip."

Henry noted the slur but didn't get riled when Rolf called Cerissa a "thing"—there was no true venom behind Rolf's tone anymore, and Henry had learned not to react to the teasing. "Do not worry. No one is dictating anything—including you. But compromise is inevitable. After what Anne-Louise put her through, now is not the time to push her boundaries about body modesty."

"I will accommodate a few things in the name of our friendship, but you can't use what happened with your maker as leverage to coddle every one of Cerissa's idiosyncrasies."

"Of course, my friend," Henry said, clapping Rolf on the shoulder. "I merely ask for some consideration."

"*Ach*, whatever. I'm going to heat some dark wine first. Do you want any?" With a sly grin, Rolf added, "I want to fully recharge by the time we leave the hot tub. I have more plans for Karen."

"Very good." Not that he'd voice it, but Henry had similar plans for Cerissa. "So let us get this party started."

Befow going outside to the covered patio, Cerissa scooted past the guys in the small kitchen. The living room, dining area, and kitchen made one big rectangle, with the kitchen demarcated by its linoleum floor and small center island. She opened a bottle of wine, and Henry wolf-whistled, eyeing her body as if the one-piece swimsuit was invisible.

Her face warmed. Sometimes showing less skin was sexier, and it covered the scars on her back, which she was still hesitant to let others see—even her friends. After pouring wine for herself and Karen, she carried the plastic glasses, leaving the bottle behind.

She placed them on the patio table, then helped Karen remove the round vinyl cover from the tub. They studied the controls and, between the two of them, figured out how to start the jet bubbles.

Cerissa sank into the hot water with a sigh, the plastic wineglass in her hand, feeling the tension from the flight easing. Bear had followed them outside, doing zoomies around the enclosed patio with a tennis ball in his mouth.

She took a sip of wine. "When do you want to work on wedding plans?"

Karen laughed. "Woah, girlfriend. Vacation just started. We'll find time. Maybe tomorrow night while the guys are skiing, if we don't feel up to staying on the slopes after dark."

Rolf appeared suddenly and vaulted into the tub with all the grace of a college student at a frat party. The wave he created drenched them, which was probably his intent.

"Rolf!" Cerissa and Karen yelled in unison, both yanking their glasses into the air to avoid getting hot tub water splashed into the wine.

Henry slid in much more gracefully.

Wiping the chlorinated water from her face, Cerissa glowered at Rolf, then asked, "So, what's the plan tomorrow with you two?"

She knew in general terms what was on the agenda. But she wasn't sure about the schedule or what the guys wanted to do.

Henry set his plastic mug on the back edge of the spa. "Have you considered a private lesson?"

When they agreed to the trip, she'd informed him she'd tried skiing over thirty years ago. So, in all reality, she was a beginner.

"I'm not against the idea."

Henry ran his hand over her arm. "I'd recommend it to start. Because of your background, list yourself as intermediate. You'll get a better instructor, and it won't matter if you aren't an intermediate skier, as you'll be alone with the instructor. Until you get back on the slopes, you can't truly assess what level you're at."

"That sounds fine."

"We can rent your skis when we book your lesson," Karen added.

Rolf raised himself to sit on the spa's flat edge and sipped his mug of dark wine. "Henry and I will be ready to leave by four twenty in the afternoon. You and Karen should plan on having an early dinner before then. We won't have much time to ski—night skiing ends at ten. We'll make it back to the base by ten thirty if we time the last lift right."

Henry squeezed Cerissa's hand. "Our helicopter skiing is the night after. We're acquainted with a vampire pilot who accommodates such requests, but we'll see if the weather cooperates. The first night, we should ski together, so I can see how comfortable you are on the slopes. If you're doing well, we may take you on a few of the difficult runs with us. But not on the helicopter."

"What Henry isn't saying," Karen added, "is that both he and Rolf have no problem conquering the double black diamond runs. I've skied most of my life, but I can't compete with them. I'm okay on black diamonds. Occasionally I'll follow them on one of the more challenging courses, but I prefer not to push the limits. I'll be just as happy on blue runs with you as I would be on black diamonds. So we can ski together and let them go off on their own."

"It's been too long since I've been on skis." Cerissa grimaced, uncomfortable that the avid skiers had suddenly focused on her inexperience. "I wouldn't know a blue from a black." Although both sounded like a good way to end up black and blue, all bruised up from falling headlong down a steep slope.

"Don't worry about it," Karen replied. "The idea is to have fun and enjoy the experience. I hope it snows while we're here. There is nothing so magical as skiing a long run when no one else is around, and the snowflakes are gently falling. The air smells so fresh and the world looks so peaceful."

"What about Bear? He's not old enough to be left on his own in a rental."

At hearing his name, the pup rose on his legs at the edge of the tub. Cerissa laughed.

"Already have you covered, girlfriend. There's a doggie daycare that's open until midnight."

"Great, thank you for researching that. I should've arranged his care before this."

The puppy pressed his front paws below the tub's edge and kicked his back feet against the side, scrambling for purchase to hoist himself over.

"No, you're not allowed in here." Henry grabbed the ball from his mouth and gave it a little toss. Bear went running after it. "As soon as we're home, we'll start obedience training with that one."

Cerissa almost sputtered out the swallow of wine she'd taken. "S-so early? He's too young."

"Don't worry, you won't have to become an expert. Just as with you and flight lessons, it'll be better to have a professional teach him."

Well, they'd see about that. She didn't appreciate the idea of some stranger training her puppy. What if they were overly harsh with him? But she didn't want to argue with Henry—not yet, and not in front of Rolf and Karen after what happened on the plane. When they returned home, she'd address it. After all, he had said the dog was all her responsibility. She wasn't going to let him snatch control away from her that easily.

But she still scratched her head over why she broke her promise to herself and bickered with Henry in the cockpit.

I just wanted to prove to him that I could do it.

Yup, that sounded about right. And he'd been on a short fuse, but she'd also pushed him. Guilt nagged at her, even though they'd already discussed the issue and come to a resolution. Did she owe him more of an apology for pushing against his instructions? She rubbed her chin. It sure felt like it.

The next time they were in private, she would. Just a straight-up apology, no rationalizations. She owed him that much.

CHAPTER 10
INDIGENOUS ANIMALS

MOUNTAIN TOP CONDOS—LATER THAT NIGHT

Henry leaned back in the bubbles, focused on his mate's bottom as she lifted herself over the rim of the hot tub. After thirty minutes of soaking, both ladies were ready to get out, and steam rose from their swimsuits into the frigid patio air. He crooked his finger in Cerissa's direction. She grabbed a towel and tiptoed over, minimizing contact with the cold deck while gooseflesh coursed over her bare skin, and kissed him.

"Strip, and meet me in the shower," he whispered.

She smiled coyly and took off, Bear trailing after her.

Once the women were out of earshot, Henry told Rolf, "Cerissa and I are taking some alone time."

"*Ja, ja.*" Rolf waved dismissively. "When they go to sleep, I'll finish connecting the video game console to the television."

"Excellent."

Rolf followed Karen into her room, and Henry checked on Bear. Cerissa had left him in his carrier in the kitchen with a chew toy and water. All set.

When he reached the bathroom, the shower was already running. He stripped off his trunks, dropped them in the sink where Cerissa's swimsuit soaked in sudsy water, and swished them around.

"I'm coming in," he warned, pulling on the glass shower door, which opened with a *click*.

Naked and wet from head to toe, Cerissa looked so inviting.

"Close the door. You're causing a draft."

She didn't need to tell him. Her perky breasts were upright, the nipples two hard points. Arousal slid straight to his *pene*, and the door clicked closed.

He leered at her. "Let me help warm you."

He poured jasmine body wash onto his palms and ran his hands over her shoulders, her arms, her stomach. The fragrance rose in the steamy air; her luscious skin was silky under his touch.

She pressed against him, rubbing her slick body on his. "I wanted to say I'm sorry about what happened on the plane," she whispered near his ear. "We found a solution, but I should have listened to you in the first place."

"All is well, *mi amor*." He stroked her back, growing harder, distracted by the feel of her. "And I could have been more patient. Besides, you can make amends to me in bed."

"Henry!" She moved back and splashed water at him, but he captured her in his arms again for a kiss hotter than the steam.

When they finished showering, he helped dry her, then carried her to bed, claiming her as his. After they made love, he cuddled her for a while.

Before she dozed off, he said, "I should check on Rolf. I promised him time with a video game."

"Hmm," she murmured sleepily. "Put Bear in the bathroom, please. I'm going to morph and doze by the fireplace."

Although initially Henry thought Bear would sleep best in the kitchen, after giving it further consideration, he decided the bathroom was a better location. Since the plan was for him and Rolf to play video games in the living room while the women slept, their voices might disturb the puppy if he slept in the kitchen.

"Of course, *mi amor*."

After pulling on sweats and a t-shirt, he cracked the door and peered around the corner to find the living room empty. Once he lugged the sleeping puppy and his gear to the bathroom, he left the door to Cerissa's room partway open and returned to find Rolf in the living room, connecting the video game system they'd brought along.

Henry went into the kitchen and filled a bowl with water and set it on the floor.

"Is that for Bear?" Rolf asked, digging into a bag to retrieve an HDMI cable.

"The water is for Cerissa. She is completing her daily morph and is lying by the fireplace in our room. If she gets thirsty, she can help herself."

"That explains why you left the door to her room partway open. Will our talking disturb her?"

"No, she's not asleep, just resting."

"All right. Want to play?"

"What game have you loaded?"

Henry eased onto the couch next to Rolf to see the television screen. It was a military combat game. They both enjoyed the realistic portrayal of the kills. The volume was low enough that it wouldn't wake Karen, but with their enhanced vampire hearing, they could clearly decipher the sounds. Switching to headsets was an option if the noise became a problem.

He peeked at his phone, tempted to tap the betting app. The gnawing of Anne-Louise's tug continued to annoy him. He opened the app and considered distracting himself by placing a sizeable bet on a soccer match currently being held in a different time zone.

"Henry?" Rolf said. "Are you playing?"

Henry sighed. "I am."

He discarded the betting app, canceling the outrageous dollar amount he'd typed in. He didn't have that kind of money to lose. Putting the phone away, he grabbed the game controller.

They'd barely started the battle mission when Cerissa stuck her nose out the doorway of her room and growled. "Everything is fine," Henry said to her. "It's just the video game. We aren't under attack."

He didn't stop defending their position, moving his hands with lightning speed across the controller.

Cerissa trotted over and sat by Henry's legs.

Rolf did a double take, and Henry laughed. Rolf had never seen her as a timber wolf before. "She makes a handsome bitch."

"She prefers to assume the shape of wildlife native to the surrounding area," Henry said, petting her head with one hand then returning to the game.

"But didn't hunters eliminate wolves from Colorado?"

"At one point. But gray wolves are back. So she figured the species an appropriate choice."

Rolf half shrugged and resumed shooting at the military invaders as he spoke. "It's unfortunate that humans destroyed their food source and then hunted them until they were all gone. What a waste of a good predator." He paused the action after he killed another player. "Wait. Can she birth a litter in that form? We would make a tidy profit selling the pups."

Henry growled. "How dare you—"

"*Ach*. Relax." Rolf punched his arm playfully. "I was just joking."

Henry scowled at his friend. He sounded like he'd meant his original question. "Don't even ask that in jest when she is around. I don't believe she understands everything we say when in animal form, or she would have become aggressive in response to such a suggestion. It's highly insulting."

To Cerissa, Henry added, "Go back to your room. Go. Now."

He pointed toward the door, not wanting her to overhear in case Rolf was stupid enough to make another disparaging comment. Cerissa trotted back into the bedroom.

"Are wolves always that furry?"

"Her winter coat. And do not worry—I paid the differential to have a pet in the room when we decided to bring Bear, so there will be no issue over her fur on the rug."

Still looking in the direction the wolf trotted, Rolf asked, "Why did she come in here?"

"The crystal connects our emotions, similar to the loyalty bond you share with Karen. She could feel me responding to the game, and thought I was under attack."

"Karen has learned to ignore it," Rolf said. "Don't you find Cerissa's reaction smothering?"

"Not really."

Rolf scrunched his pale brows. "Has Bear seen her as a wolf?"

"I do not believe so."

"It may be interesting when he does."

They resumed playing the video game, continuing until it was almost dawn. Rolf rose to his feet and stretched. "I'm going to bed. See you at dusk."

Being the younger vampire, he retired first. Henry used the extra time to check his email. After responding to the last business-related one, he glanced at the onslaught of messages from Anne-Louise in his inbox and ignored them. He wanted a relaxing trip, and his maker was never conducive to that. Finished, he closed the laptop and went to Cerissa's room to say goodnight to her.

She'd morphed into human form and was asleep in bed, her wavy hair mussed from tossing and turning in her sleep. He found her wild air quite appealing. Smoothing the strands back, he kissed her cheek.

"Hi there," she said, opening her eyes.

"It's close to dawn. I'm going to brush my teeth."

"All right. Kiss me again before you go to sleep."

"I do not want to wake you."

"Don't worry. I've slept long enough."

Gazing through the bathroom window revealed it was still dark. A low cloud cover must have shielded the coming sunrise.

He brushed his teeth, then untied his ponytail, combing his hair straight. Bear whined at him, watching from his bed. "Go back to sleep," he whispered to the puppy.

The bathroom door opened. Cerissa had thrown on sweats. "I'll take him outside for a pee break." She kissed Henry. "He's still not accustomed to sleeping a full night."

"Very good. Have fun skiing today."

"I'll see you later."

She clipped the leash to the puppy's harness and headed for the front door. Henry couldn't help leaving eye tracks on her. He loved her with all his heart, and the care she showed for the pup continued to warm his heart. He went into the third bedroom, and as he lay on the bottom bunk bed, he sank into darkness to visions of her.

CHAPTER 11
PROBLEM SOLVED

SNOWSTONE MOUNTAIN—LATE MORNING

"This way," Karen announced over her shoulder, skiing away fast, making perfect S curves over the slope before pulling to the side of the run and elegantly spraying powder.

Cerissa skied off the chairlift, catching an edge of her skis as she curved down the steep ramp, raising one leg, trying to regain balance. Plopping the airborne ski onto the snow, she crossed tails and almost fell, then slid out of control. To avoid the line of trees beyond the trail's drop-off, she dug into a snowplow, an upside-down V-shape, torturing her thigh muscles with the pressure she applied. She managed to stop near Karen without falling on her butt or smashing into a tall, thick pine. A win!

"Good job," Karen said. "This is a beginner run. You might as well try it before your lesson begins."

"I'm less sure about this than I was last night. I may have previously cross-country skied, not downhill."

"Don't let the slope stress you. Just use the wedge position to get to the base and back in line for the lift. If you can, try turning, alternating directions. But if you can't, you can always snowplow straight down this run. It's almost flat here."

"If you say so." It didn't feel flat to Cerissa. If anything, the slope descended like a sharp cliff.

She pushed off with her poles to get going and made it about halfway to the bottom before falling. Karen gracefully skied to where Cerissa lay, coming to a fast stop, showering her with icy powder.

"Turn your skis perpendicular to the slope, dig your pole tips into the downhill side, and push to lift yourself."

Cerissa struggled to get upright, but then started moving forward unexpectedly, heading toward the pine trees and ungroomed snow that bordered the ski run. She fell to one side to keep from slamming into a hard trunk.

Wiping the melting crystals from her goggles, she huffed. "That didn't work very well."

"It takes time to learn. Flip your skis around to point the other way. It's easier to do when you're still on the ground."

"All right, I'll try it." Cerissa eventually lifted one ski, and then the other, positioning them in the correct direction. Karen offered the handle of one ski pole, which Cerissa grabbed and, with her friend tugging on the other end, managed to stand and stay upright.

"Okay, bestie. Go forward."

This time, Cerissa got into the wedge before she started moving downhill. By the time she was at the base, her thighs burned, and she had no strength left. Karen adroitly stopped next to her, making it appear easy.

It wasn't. "I'm using muscles I haven't used before, others in ways I've never used them."

"You'll be glad we have the hot tub tonight."

That was an understatement. "My lesson starts in about forty minutes. Do we have time to eat lunch? I'm going to need all the energy I can get to make it through."

"Sure. Pop off your skis and we can leave them in the racks."

Over a meal of chili and cornbread on the outdoor patio, the weak sunlight warming her back, Cerissa raised the question she'd put off asking. On the one hand, she'd been afraid to trigger Karen's PTSD. They'd had a very brief exchange at the party about the Cutter's resurrection as a vampire and final death, but then Jayden's drama the next day pushed it from her mind. On the other hand, it only felt right to check in with how her friend was feeling.

"We didn't get to finish our conversation on Christmas Eve. About what happened in New York."

Karen made a face, then bit into her cornbread, which was slathered generously with honey butter. "So?"

"Have you spoken to Fidelia about it?"

"We talked a little." Fidelia was the Lux therapist assigned to Karen's case. Karen couldn't talk to the Hill's resident therapist, not with all the secrets she held in her head. "I'm okay, really, I am. It's a relief to know the Cutter's dead now and can't hurt anyone else. What about you?"

"Glad we rescued Rick. Allison seems to have adapted to envoy life and is dating Warren. Anne-Louise released Henry. And Tig and Jayden seem willing to keep our secret. The only problem I have right now is I can't ski."

Karen laughed. "Yeah, I saw."

"It's a real dilemma. If I learn how to ski the way a human learns, it'll be years before I'm as proficient as you are."

"I figured you'd master it more quickly. You have certain natural, ah, advantages," Karen said, spreading more honey butter on her corn bread.

"Only if I draw on them."

"Why wouldn't you use them?"

"Well, I'd need to morph to match a body that had ski memory."

"In English?"

"If I morphed to mimic a woman who was an expert skier and then skied in that body, I'd have the advantage of her muscle memory to practice how to take the slopes. Then, when I morphed back to me, I could change my muscles to retain the skill, while keeping my own external appearance."

"Morph to match me. You've done it before."

"To save lives. Not to soothe my ego."

"Hey, I don't mind. Although I'm not an expert. But you'll improve your skiing if your theory works, and then we can all ski together tonight. I can tell you Henry and Rolf will have no patience if you force them to stay on the green runs. Not to mention, it's better than picking some stranger, morphing to look like them, and then running into them on a lift."

Cerissa chuckled. Yeah, she could picture the horror on a skier's face if they suddenly found they had a doppelgänger. And tonight, all the gang would have more fun if her skiing improved. Maybe Karen was right.

"If I do this, I'll only do it for the lesson, so we won't need to tell anyone. It helps that we're basically the same size. These stretch ski pants can accommodate the fact I'm curvier and you're taller."

"Well, go ahead, then."

"Right here?"

"No one is watching." Karen said with a scoff. "And if they are, they won't believe it. They'll discount their own eyes."

Cerissa glanced around and noticed the arrow pointing to the women's room. "I'm going to find a more private place. Be right back."

It only took a few minutes to locate an available stall in the bathroom, and, keeping only her own hair color, she morphed into Karen's form. Making customizations to a body she'd mapped was hard, and of all the modifications she might make, hair color was the easiest. This way, they passed for sisters rather than identical twins.

When she returned and clunked to the table in her ski boots, Karen said, "So that's how I'd look with dark brown hair. No thanks. I'll stay the auburn I am. It's more attractive with my skin tone."

Cerissa laughed. "I better go take that lesson now."

She carried her tray over, dumped the empty paper bowl and plate into the trash can, and left the tray on the stack next to it. Even walking in clunky ski boots was easier. Her feet didn't slip on the slick deck, and her confidence spiked. She glanced over at Karen, who added her empty tray to the pile. "This really makes a difference. I now see how you move in the gear."

"Good. I'll meet you back here after your lesson is over." Karen put an arm around Cerissa, gave her a hug goodbye, then stepped away, cringing. "That felt weird. I've read those self-help books about giving yourself a hug, but I never took it literally before. Bye for now."

Cerissa grabbed her skis and clomped over to the meetup signs for classes. Her instructor turned out to be a nice blond guy with a skier's tan. On the ski lift, they talked about her experience—really, Karen's experience.

Her lesson went extremely well. The instructor expressed surprise she'd labeled herself "intermediate." By the end of the three hours, she'd skied the advanced black diamond terrain she'd heard her friends talk about. The instructor helped her fine-tune her technique, and she now knew what mistakes Karen made.

Maybe she'd pass on the tips to Karen. It was the least she could do for her bestie.

With the private instruction over, Cerissa boarded a chairlift by herself. Alone in the air, she put her wind mask on to hide the process, then morphed back to Cerissa, but kept the muscle memory. When she skied off the lift, she felt confident, and gracefully cut a tight S shape as she glided down the center of the slope.

Karen skied up behind her. "Wow!"

"You saw me?"

"The way you took that last run—yes, I did. What a difference a lesson makes."

"It wasn't the lesson, bestie. I couldn't have done it without your help. Thank you for lending me your body."

"My pleasure."

"You should consider scheduling a class this week. The instructor really helped me on the moguls. Or I could pass on his tips, if you prefer."

"Maybe. I followed a bit to check out what he was showing you. So let me practice on my own tonight when the guys join us and go from there." Karen made a face. "But it was weird watching myself ski."

Cerissa laughed, then pointed downhill with her pole. "Let's go into town and grab dinner before the guys wake."

"Works for me."

By the time they finished eating, collected Bear, and got back to the condo, an uneasy, icy feeling invaded Cerissa's chest. She stomped the snow off her boots and then shut the door behind her.

From the couch, Henry *harrumphed*.

"What's wrong?" She unsnapped Bear's leash, and he made a beeline for the toy box.

The men were in the living room, dressed, and, from the empty mugs in the sink, had fed.

"Aside from you and Karen getting back late?" He aimed his gaze at his Patek Philippe watch. "I need to rent my skis before the shop closes."

She ignored his crankiness and refused to take the bait. "Yes, aside from that."

They were only tardy by a few minutes, since they'd had to retrieve Bear from the dog-sitter and listen to the woman gush over how he'd been the bestest boy. Right now, the puppy wrestled with a stuffie—and it looked like the stuffie was winning. They'd feed him and then drop him off again at the sitter's on the way back to the mountain.

Cerissa opened his puppy chow and poured half a cup. At the sound, Bear abandoned the stuffie and came charging, scrambling for purchase on the vinyl flooring in the kitchen. At his weight and age, he received four small meals every day.

Watching the puppy inhale his chow, she didn't believe being late was the real problem. They'd be ready to go in minutes.

"Henry?"

He ran his hands through his hair. It was hanging loose about his shoulders; he hadn't tied it back yet. "Anne-Louise left me a message demanding I phone her back. I will wait until later."

"Then what's wrong?"

"Even though she has contractually agreed to release the blood bond, it will linger for nine months, more or less, from her last feeding. She last bit me in May. I have at least another month or two before it fades permanently."

"So?"

"I can feel her tugging at the bond. Incessantly. Her call is weak now, which is why I can easily disobey it, but I find her tugs rather annoying."

"I'm sorry." No wonder he was in a foul mood. "Wait. How long has she been doing that?"

"Since I ignored her first message before we left for the airport."

Aha. "Is that why you were so grumpy on the plane?"

He glared at her.

Maybe she should have kept that thought to herself. "Can you ignore it?"

"I plan on doing so."

She walked over to where he still sat on the couch and hugged him. "Then relax and enjoy the trip, all right?"

"Of course, *cariña mia*." He kissed her.

"Are you two going to sit around playing kissy-face all evening?" Rolf hovered over them with his skis in hand.

"No, Rolf," Henry replied. "There will be plenty of time later for that."

Cerissa ignored the other grumpy vampire in the room, plucked the leather thong from Henry's fingers, and tied his ponytail for him.

Rolf thumped his hard plastic ski boot against the floor. "Then let's go. *Schnell*. Get the lead out."

Bear, having licked his bowl clean, barked at the noise and attacked Rolf's boot, who grabbed the pup's harness to stop him.

Karen sneaked behind Rolf and slipped her arms around him. "We better get moving before he gets his knickers in a twist."

"Be quiet, *Fraulein*. I'll take no disrespect from you." He released Bear and turned to kiss her. "Now let's go."

Once they dropped off Bear, and Henry rented his skis, he insisted on Cerissa joining them for a couple of runs. She went along with it. When the four of them got back on the quad lift, Henry said, "I'm quite impressed. For someone out of practice, your form is perfect on the intermediate slopes."

Cerissa exchanged knowing glances with Karen. "I had a great instructor."

"Do you feel up to trying a black diamond?" Rolf asked.

"Sure. I was on the blacks for a while with the instructor."

"Excellent."

The evening wind blew stronger than during the daytime, and the chairlift swayed on the heavy steel cable that carried them above the treetops. Cerissa quickly gripped the safety bar.

"Do not worry," Henry said. "We're safe."

It was a bit of a drop—almost two stories. She raised her eyes to the sky instead and took a deep, cleansing breath.

The night air was crisp, with only a few clouds drifting overhead. Stars lit the field of black. The full moon illuminated the mountain peak above them. A light dusting of white crystals covered the pine trees, and ahead of them, a squirrel ran down the trunk of one tree to hop on a nearby branch, sending a shower of snow falling to the ground. She could even hear the crunchy sound of skiers gliding over the icy slopes. After melting slightly during the day, the snow's fluffy powder refroze as night temperatures dropped, making the surface icier.

Henry pointed to an area where the mountain created the shape of a bowl. "See Independence Bowl, to the southeast? On the wilderness side is where we'll helicopter ski. They have access by snowcats during the day, but at night, we can only reach the ridge by helicopter."

"Why?"

"It's too dangerous for mortals at night, so the mountain resort doesn't offer it."

"But not too dangerous for you to ski?"

"Bah," Rolf said. "It's perfectly safe. We've had no problems in the past."

Henry squeezed her gloved hand. "Rolf is right. The pilot who flies us is masterful at what he does. He would not put us on the mountain if there was any actual risk."

Skepticism rattled through her, but Henry was an experienced skier, unlike herself. She was sure that with more practice came less trepidation. "Okay, Quique."

Henry raised the safety bar as they approached the operator's cabin. "We're almost at the top. Remember to lift your ski tips before we get off."

She didn't need his coaching, but let it go. Although "bossykins" might become her new nickname for him if he continued to tell her what to do.

The four of them skied together for about an hour. Cerissa enjoyed following Henry on the black diamonds—his form was perfect, his long, lean body bouncing around the moguls in a regular rhythm, and his tight, sexy ass hugged by the stretchy ski pants.

But she also sensed she was holding the guys back. Rolf expressed his desire to try the double black diamonds, but her skill level wasn't a match for the trail's steepness.

"I'm out," she said. "I'll catch the long run to the bottom of the mountain and wait for you at the base resort's bar."

Karen chuckled. "Me too. I'm cold and tired." She waved the guys off. "Have fun. Come get us when they kick you out."

CHAPTER 12

TEMPER, TEMPER

SNOWSTONE SKI RESORT—FORTY MINUTES LATER

Henry seated himself on the ski lift next to Rolf as it swept them up and over the machinery, lightly swinging the chair. They'd completed three runs on their own and chatted about winery business, and then Henry's phone rang. He passed over his poles to Rolf so he could remove a glove and get the phone out without dropping the device. If they dropped anything in the wilderness below, they would lose it until the spring thaw—at which point it'd be worthless.

If someone was calling him, it had to be important. He'd left word at the winery that he didn't want to be disturbed, and he'd set Anne-Louise's number to go straight to voicemail. A quick glance at the screen confirmed the number belonged to his attorney, Marcus Collings. He swiped accept.

"Marcus, we are on a ski lift, so I cannot talk for long." Then it occurred to him—he'd put his vampire child under the care of Marcus and Zeke while he was gone. "Is Christine all right?"

"She's fine. Since you're short on time, I'll get to the point. Anne-Louise phoned me. She's pissed and demanding that I tell her where you are."

"*Madre de Dios*. What does she want that's so urgent it can't wait until my vacation is over?"

"She wants you to attend the wedding rehearsal dinner."

The *puta* was calling his lawyer and pulling at the bond over this idiocy? Hot anger simmered in his veins.

"And why would I attend the rehearsal? We are not in the wedding party."

"She wants her children to give her away."

Henry groaned. Loudly. "When is it?"

"The night before the wedding."

"Of all the selfish things to do, to ask at the last minute, when we were at her engagement party two weeks ago. Now, we'll have to cut our vacation short, and I won't ask Rolf to do that."

"Do you want me to tell her?"

"No. And do not tell her where I am. Thank you. Goodnight."

Henry contained his anger through the end of the call. Then he hauled back and threw the phone with all his strength against the snow-dusted rocks below them, and stared as the lift swung past it. At least the temptation to place an online bet was no longer an option. His friend and bookie, Petar Petrov, operated the betting app and it only worked on his phone.

"That was mature," Rolf said. "Feel better?"

"Do not mock me. That was Marcus—"

"I heard the whole thing. What do you want to do?"

"I won't ask you to cut the trip short."

"If you want us to, it's okay. There will be other ski trips."

The chairlift approached the station. Henry moved his skis off the footrest, lifted the safety bar, and zoomed ahead of Rolf, choosing the ski run leading to the most difficult terrain. He barreled down it with no regard for his own welfare.

When they got to the base of the mountain resort, Rolf said, "Why don't we quit for the night?"

"But we have at least another hour left to ski."

"You keep skiing like that and you're going to break something, and then you'll lose a full night's skiing, if not more."

Rage filled Henry's chest, then he tamped down the fire crackling through him. "You are right. I'm preoccupied by Marcus's call. I want to ski another run, and if you're still concerned afterward, we'll quit for the night."

"Fair enough. But if you break something, I won't stop skiing to nursemaid you."

"Agreed. Besides, Cerissa can perform that function."

As they got in line for the next lift, Rolf's phone rang. "Hello, *Liebling*."

Henry leaned in to eavesdrop on both ends of the conversation.

"Hi, babe. Cerissa and I are tired. We're going back to the condo. How are you guys doing?"

"We're about to get on the lift again. Where are you?"

"Waiting for the shuttle. We'll collect Bear and meet you at the condo."

"Take the van. It'll be easier to get the dog. Henry and I will catch the shuttle."

"You sure? It stops running at ten forty-five."

"We'll make it on time, don't worry."

"Okay, thanks. If I fall asleep, wake me when you get in?"

"You can count on it. Any particular way you want me to wake you?"

"Be creative," Karen replied, laughing. "Bye for now."

Henry's face warmed. Perhaps he shouldn't have eavesdropped.

Rolf clicked off the call. "The women are returning to the condo. When we're finished, we'll meet them there."

"Please say nothing to Karen or Cerissa about Anne-Louise. I do not want her nonsense to cloud our trip. Despite your kind offer, I'm not sure I'll pander to her wishes and cut our vacation short."

"That's awkward," Rolf said as they shuffled forward. There weren't that many skiers on the slopes this late, so the queue moved quickly. "Karen will not be happy if you decide to leave early and I spring it on her at the last minute."

"I thought you didn't let your mate dictate what you do."

"I don't let *your* mate dictate what I'll do. Karen is a different issue."

They shuffled to the loading line, and the chairlift swung underneath them. Henry lowered the safety bar to rest his skis on the footrests—he didn't like dangling them.

"You exaggerate how important it is for her to learn now," Henry replied. "And I would prefer Cerissa not know anything. Her instinct is to keep the peace. She'll want to cave in and agree to Anne-Louise's demands. I want more time to consider the matter, and if you tell Karen, she will tell Cerissa."

"Why do I suspect your desire for secrecy has something to do with the fact you smashed your phone on the face of the mountain?"

"Perhaps." He'd worked so hard to control his anger. But Anne-Louise had this way of aggravating him despite all the work he'd done with Father Matt. It felt like two steps backward for every step forward. "Cerissa does not need to hear I lost my temper that way. It will only make her more worried. I'll order a new phone tonight, and the replacement will arrive before I wake tomorrow."

"You pander to her too much."

"And you do not pander to Karen?"

"Point taken. I'll keep your secret for now. But if you decide to cut things a day short, they'll have to be told."

"That is self-evident."

Henry raised the safety bar, and as soon as they reached the chairlift's disembarkation point, Rolf skied ahead, grabbing the lead and shouting over his shoulder. "Just don't wait until the last minute."

Mountain Top Condos—Around the same time

Cerissa had her head close to Karen's as they both stared at the laptop's screen. A wedding planner website told her how far behind she and Henry were in planning their important day. Karen had done the initial work of creating an account for Cerissa on the site. It provided a place to store all the details while giving each of them access to the information so they could collaborate. Even Henry had his own login.

Karen patted Cerissa's leg. "Don't panic. We have enough time to plan your wedding. Have you set the date yet?"

"We were talking about a year from our engagement, which would be the end of August or beginning of September. But that also puts it in the middle of harvest season. Henry suggested moving the date to October, so he has time to supervise loading the grapes into the vats."

"I get it—William's an extraordinary assistant winemaker, but Henry's a control freak."

"And I need to check with Nicholas to see if he and Marcus picked a date yet."

"True. Though you got engaged first, so you have first pick. That's the rule on the Hill."

"Whatever." Cerissa shrugged. "And in Hindu tradition, we need to select an auspicious date and time."

"A what?"

Cerissa chuckled. "There are entire books defining the concept and how to calculate it. Think of it as avoiding dates and times with bad mojo. October can be problematic, but there are ways around it. Even having all the family and guests present declare the time auspicious works as a last-ditch effort."

Karen frowned at her. "I kind of understood that."

"Don't worry, I'll vet the date after Henry weighs in with his choices. But that only gives us ten months. I bought my wedding sari already, and we're going to hold the event at our home..."

"You could use the winery."

"We did that for the engagement party."

With money tight, Cerissa didn't expect Henry to be happy over the additional cost of reserving the winery. Even though her family was paying for the wedding, she just knew if she picked the winery, Henry wouldn't let them pay. And since he co-owned the winery, if they took over a rental ballroom for an evening without paying, that meant lost income to both partners.

Hmm. His issues around money were still something they needed to work on.

Their trip to New York had been possible because they stayed in a guest apartment at the Collective for free, thanks to her sponsor. Leopold was doing the same for them again when they attended Anne-Louise's wedding. Rolf was covering the remaining expenses for this trip. But she didn't want to mention the financial concerns to Karen. Henry was quite sensitive about them.

She bit her lip, deciding to keep her explanation simple. "We wanted a different venue for the wedding, to make it a smaller, more intimate event. With the engagement party, we invited the entire Hill. For the wedding—"

"What about the Hill's country club?"

"If we booked their ballroom, wouldn't we have to include everyone who lives on the Hill? I don't want the mean vampires as guests—"

"Oh, sweetie, you don't have to invite anyone you don't want to. It's your wedding."

"Good. I'm not ready to extend the olive branch."

"You invite who you want. We're your friends. We'll support you and cheer you and Henry past the finish line."

"Thanks."

Karen played with a strand of her auburn hair. "But you're right. You can probably limit the number of guests more easily with a home wedding, as you originally suggested." She paused, a look of consideration on her face. "What do you say about using our house? Henry's drawing room is suitable for small, intimate parties. When Rolf built our house, he planned it for grand gatherings. That way, you can invite who you want, and not worry about having room."

"But I don't want you doing all that work."

"Don't worry. It won't be like the Christmas party. I'll hire a caterer to provide everything—tables, chairs, linens, food and drink, the works. When we get home, we can visit my favorites to taste-test their menus."

"Do you think Rolf will agree?"

The smug grin on Karen's face said it all. "He'll agree. He owes me *Drachenfutter* from prior screw-ups. So let's enter our house into the app—at a minimum, it can act as a placeholder until you and Henry decide."

Cerissa recognized the German word for dragon food—compensation to the angry dragon at home when the other mate made a major blunder. And from what Karen had told her in the past, Rolf owed plenty.

Karen typed the location into the wedding planner. Cerissa groaned. There were still a bajillion decisions left to make.

"Next—your guestlist."

"Why do I need that so early?"

"To mail the 'save the date' cards."

"Mine won't be too long. I have to invite Leopold and include his plus-one, although he's not dating anyone right now." He was her business partner and sponsor among the vampire communities, after all. She'd also have to include a few Lux friends and dignitaries. They'd appear in human form for the ceremony. "In total, there'll be about ten people on my side."

"Seriously? You must have more friends and family than that."

"Hmm. Besides Leopold? From among the Lux... My cousin Ari, of course, and my mother. I'll probably extend an invitation to the head of the Lux, Agathe, but I doubt she'll attend. I have a few close nest mates and friends. Everyone I met in medical school is on the East Coast, but more importantly, given the Hill's nature, I'm not inviting mortals I haven't seen in five years. Why take the risk of having strangers around?"

Karen changed browser tabs to the blank fields for the guestlist. "Well, let's type in those you know right now."

Cerissa took the laptop back and entered the names. "The remainder will be Hill residents or other friends of Henry's. At least twenty who I'm close with too. We'll overlap there."

"Then that makes it easier. Why don't you type in the rest, and when the guys get back, Henry can fill in his part of the list before dawn? There's a fantastic online printer who will print and send these for you. The vendor even addresses the envelopes using calligraphy. So once the guests are inked, you're almost done with that phase."

"But the location isn't finalized yet. You need to confirm with Rolf, and Henry has to weigh in."

"The save-the-dates don't need a location beyond 'Sierra Escondida,' so you can keep it vague."

"Good." Cerissa glanced at the endless advance preps schedule and shifted in her seat. "What do I do about Ari and Gaea? My cousin isn't famous for long-term relationships."

"Give me a second." Karen searched for something on her phone. "Got it. Send an invitation to each, but skip adding 'and guest' on the invitation. If they break up, you can informally extend the plus-one offer."

"All right, we can do that."

"Okay, next section. Who's going to be in the wedding party?"

"Ah, Father Matt will conduct the service. He said he'd study the Hindu rituals I want to include." Cerissa turned to face Karen. "And I want you for my maid of honor—if you'd be willing?"

Karen squealed and hugged her. "Yes, I'd love that! We're going to have so much fun! Who else is a bridesmaid?"

"I want to keep it simple—no other bridesmaids, assuming Henry can keep his groomsmen to one." Cerissa pursed her lips. "And before you ask, because I know it's your next question, you can choose any dress you want so long as it's blue. It's the color of sacredness in Hinduism. I've always pictured my bridesmaid in royal blue, but you can select any shade that works for you."

"Royal blue is perfect. Any style?"

"There are Indian dressmakers online that'll give you ideas if you want to try something different—some pretty elegant Bollywood styles. And you remember the restaurant we've eaten at, the House of India? Well, there are two clothing stores on that block, which sell wedding saris and other formalwear. They serve the small population that lives in Mordida and dresses traditionally. But if you prefer an American full-length formal, that's fine too."

"Got it. And best man?"

"Henry hasn't told me yet." Cerissa's throat tightened. "If Yacov was still with us, I suspect he would be Henry's choice. I'll ask him later tonight."

"Okay, I won't say anything to Rolf. Do you have a ring bearer or flower girl?"

"Um, no one I'm close to."

"Well, by next October, Bear will be a year old and trained. What do you say to using him?"

At the mention of his name, Bear came running from the kitchen, where he'd been gnawing on a teething dinosaur. Cerissa laughed and threw the dinosaur for him to chase.

"Fine. Enter his name for now." She sighed. "How many more of these decisions are there? I'm feeling overwhelmed by it all."

"Then we'll stop for now. This is supposed to be fun." Karen closed the laptop and took another sip of wine. "Once we're home, you'll want to carve out time to visit florists, do the cake testing, and shop for wedding rings."

Cerissa fanned her fingers, displaying the elegant ring she wore. They'd agreed to add a nesting gold band, since it was an expensive three-diamond affair, with a flawless center stone Yacov had cut and sold to Henry before his death. "Oh my Goddess, I haven't purchased Henry's band yet. He said to keep his ring simple, but I want something elegant for him."

"I know just the jeweler. Don't worry, we can grab some time together during the day to go shopping, and then you can give him his options."

The front door opened, and Bear made a mad charge, barking furiously at the intruders.

"Oh, shut up," Rolf grumbled at the dog.

"Bear, here, boy." When he didn't come, Cerissa rushed over to hoist him into the air, gave Henry a quick kiss, and then pulled the little daybed over by the couch, putting the puppy by her feet. "Stay."

That lasted all of ten seconds.

"You guys are back earlier than planned."

"Not by much," Henry replied, leaning his skis against the pegged rack in the entryway and bringing Bear back to her.

She lifted the dog onto her lap and snuggled him close.

"Cerissa, he is not a lapdog. You will spoil him if you keep doing that. When he's too big to fit, what will you do?"

Okay, her mate sounded cranky again, and his mood washed through the crystal, bordering somewhere between irritated and angry. And that was despite the muting bracelet he wore.

He'd been fine when they skied together. What had happened on the slopes after she left?

She continued holding Bear in her lap, ignoring his comment. "How was the skiing?"

"Excellent," Rolf replied. "Good powder where they haven't groomed, and they've opened more black diamond runs for night skiing."

"How about you, Quique? Did you have fun?"

Henry sat next to her on the couch and gave her another quick kiss. "Yes, I did."

Karen furrowed her brow as she rose to her feet and grimaced at him. "That doesn't sound very convincing."

Before Henry could reply, Karen sauntered over to greet Rolf, who'd gone into the kitchen to heat a pouch of dark wine.

"We would have liked more time on the mountain, that's all." Rolf curled an arm around his mate and, after receiving a kiss, added with a leer, "I'm both pleased and disappointed to find you awake."

"Oh?"

"I've been thinking of all the creative ways to wake you the entire bus ride back."

Karen smiled widely at that. "There's always tomorrow."

Cerissa stifled a giggle and wondered if her friends would always play an endless game of innuendo.

Henry squeezed Cerissa's hand. "I'm going to shower. Then I want to check my email."

"We've been working on wedding plans," Cerissa called after him, but got no response. "Could you please enter your guestlist into the website tonight? I sent you the link."

He didn't stop to answer, and the bedroom door closed behind him.

Karen wrinkled her nose at Rolf and motioned for him to go. "You need to shower, too. We're going to open the champagne and celebrate New Year's Eve early while you two get clean."

"Don't get too drunk, *Liebling*. I have plans."

Karen laughed at him. "You always do."

Cerissa tried not to let the emotions emanating from Henry spoil her mood. After popping the cork and toasting the New Year, she tried a second round of wedding planning. The brief break energized her—or maybe it was the champagne—and the feeling of being overwhelmed lifted. Now, she just wanted to get more of the forms completed. Ever the planner, Karen clapped her hands in delight and joined Cerissa on the couch.

As they made progress, she found the process a little easier.

When Henry returned to the living room, clean and comfortably dressed in sweats and a t-shirt, his mood hadn't improved. The flavor of it reminded her of the first night in New York, when Anne-Louise upset him with her offer to release him from the blood bond.

Had his maker done something else besides tugging on the bond and leaving voicemails? Anne-Louise was the only one who could get under Henry's skin so easily. And during the week between their return from

New York and this trip to Colorado, Henry had kept two appointments with Father Matt. She suspected Anne-Louise had been the reason.

Rolf opened the door of Karen's bedroom, and the hinge squeaked. Cerissa glanced up from where she huddled over the open laptop to see him peer into the living room.

"You." He pointed at Karen next to her, then crooked his finger. "In here."

Karen giggled. "That's my cue." She grinned at Cerissa. "Tell me tomorrow if you make any progress on the guestlist."

After they disappeared into Karen's room, Henry returned to the couch with his laptop. Cerissa swiveled hers so he could see the screen. "We've been wedding planning. Do you want to see?"

"Maybe later."

A pain tightly cinched her chest. Didn't he care about their wedding? He'd heartily agreed to share in planning all the events. Why the sudden brush-off?

She bit her lip. *Maybe it's not about me. Maybe it's about whatever was bothering him when he arrived home.*

She decided not to take his response personally. But should she ask about it? She shook her head—now wasn't the right time. When he was ready, he'd talk about it.

She stood and strode to the bedroom. "Then I'm going to morph. Come on, Bear."

The puppy followed her into the en suite bathroom, and she removed her contact lenses. She hated the slight shock generated each time she removed them, but hated even more the unrestful way they connected to a non-human eyeball. She morphed into her wolf form. Bear accepted the transformation with a few excited barks. Then he curled next to her by the fireplace in her room.

She enjoyed the canine mind, which helped lift her mood. She felt more dedicated, more loyal to Henry—not that she wasn't already, but this form amped the feeling higher. And she felt protective. Very protective. The only thing she didn't like was how sensitive her senses were—she could hear and smell Karen and Rolf having sex two rooms away. It made the fur rise on the back of her neck.

Henry opened the bedroom door and knelt by her. "You do not mind, do you?"

She sat up and tilted her head, unsure what he meant, and let her eyes ask the question.

"That we are not currently doing the same activity?" he added.

She licked his face in reply.

"Stop that. No licking." He placed a hand on her muzzle and gently pushed it away. He stroked her head and gave her a hug. It had a calming effect, to spend time with him when she was in wolf form. Reassured all was well between them, she settled down and snoozed.

CHAPTER 13

BRAT

MOUNTAIN TOP CONDOS—LATER THAT NIGHT

When she morphed back to human, the motion woke Bear, who lazily stirred and stretched. His time at daycare had done a decent job of draining his excess energy, not to mention it was wonderful for his socialization. He'd received all his vaccinations for his age, so being around other dogs wasn't a problem.

She threw on sweats and her ski jacket then hooked his leash to his harness, and the puppy came wide awake. Leading Bear to the living room, she blew Henry a kiss. Her mate was sprawled on the couch, his attention split—half watching a movie, and half typing on his laptop.

Hope shot through her. "Are you filling in the guestlist?"

"Not yet. Maybe in a few nights."

"Okay. I'll be right back."

I will not take it personally, she repeated to herself, multiple times.

The night air sent a chill through her the minute she stepped outdoors. It didn't seem to bother Bear. He tugged at the leash, investigating the juniper bushes.

After what they'd gone through in New York, she almost expected the puppy to discover a corpse there. Fortunately, that wasn't the case.

"Come on, you know why we're here. Do your business." After he finally peed, she corralled him and carried him back indoors. She'd had enough of frigid weather.

While she hung her jacket, Bear paused in the kitchen to lap at his water bowl, then made a beeline to Henry. "Say goodnight. I'm going to put him in his crate with his favorite blanket and stuffie. That seems to settle him the best."

Henry *tsked* and brushed his hands over his pant leg. "My sweats are now covered in dog slobber."

She couldn't restrain her smile. "He likes you."

Just wait until she had a baby, and he had to deal with spit-up on his shoulder. As much as Henry longed for his own children—and expressed resentment that becoming vampire made that impossible—the reality of raising a child was an entirely distinct thing from the fantasy.

She swept up the puppy, cradling him on his back. "Come on, before Henry decides it's not too late to return you to Rolf."

She buried her nose in the puppy's sweet fur and blew a raspberry. Once he was on his dog bed and snoozing again, with his water bowl refilled, she closed the bathroom door.

Now, to care for her mate.

She'd always envisioned anger as a hot emotion, but the crystal translated it as being dunked in ice cold water. Since morphing back to human, she couldn't miss the icy displeasure bubbling at her through the crystal, and it wasn't just dog slobber that had Henry mad.

From the bedroom doorway, she studied him. Sprawled on the couch, his expression serious and shut down, he didn't seem in the mood to explain.

At least he was restraining himself better than he had in New York when he had barked angry orders in response to Anne-Louise's games.

Appreciating the change in his approach, she considered different tactics to help him exercise his anger. She didn't want to force him to talk if he wasn't ready. But there were other ways to distract him...

"Hi there. What are you working on?"

He quickly folded his laptop computer, stopping her from seeing the screen. "Hello, *querida*. A small matter arose, and I've resolved it."

"That's good, because if I didn't know better, I'd say you were sitting here brooding about something."

"I do not brood."

"Yes, you do." She bent over to run her fingers along his ponytail, then played with the end, toying with ways to wrest him from his dark mood.

He narrowed his eyes at her. "And don't even think of pulling it."

"Who, me? Would I do anything so annoying as tugging on your ponytail?"

He gripped her hips and, with a quick spin, brought her bottom onto his lap, and she released his hair as he did so. "Yes, you would."

"It's nice to see you stop brooding." Of course, if he returned to his moodiness, she could easily grab the tail again to tease him.

"Have you forgotten there is a penalty for saying I brood?"

His pupils dilated, turning his eyes almost solid black as his long fingers peeled back her sweatshirt. He ducked the cool, soft tips under the fabric to run across her bare skin, tickling her.

Oops. She was in trouble now, and tried tickling him back, but he had the advantage over her—his shirt was tucked into his sweatpants, and she struggled to free it but failed.

Laughing, she tightened her elbows against her sides to defend herself from the onslaught of his fingertips. It wasn't working. "All right, I give up."

"Do you really?" He continued to glide his fingers over her ribcage, heading for her breasts.

She laughed so hard she couldn't get the words out. "Y-yes, r-really."

"Very well. I accept your surrender."

He leaned her back, positioning her to be kissed. She stopped giggling long enough for his lips to capture hers, for his tongue to claim her mouth. She gave back as good as she got until she ran short of breath and broke from him, panting.

He surged to his feet, an arm around her back and the other under her knees, then threw her over his shoulder pirate-style, and she squeaked at the abrupt way he seized her.

"Hey," she whisper-yelled, and her root chakra woke with a sizzle. Anticipation buzzed straight through her from crown to toes.

"I have not finished your punishment for saying I brood." He seductively squeezed her butt.

She grabbed his ponytail and gently pulled. If she was going to get punished, she'd get the full measure of her misbehavior.

"Brat," he mumbled.

Brat? He'd never called her that before. Was the nickname a good thing or a bad thing?

With a big smile on her face, she tugged again.

He closed the bedroom door behind them. The spank that came was half expected, and if she had to admit it to herself, the slap was so gentle, her sweatpants cushioned the light sting. A tingle ran across her skin and merged with the excitement sparking through her.

But she kicked her legs in protest nonetheless. She couldn't let him get away with manhandling her.

"Stop that," he said with another swat. "You forget, it is my turn to choose, and if you aren't careful, I'll start by pinking that delectable bottom of yours."

"Oh, I'm so worried." She tugged at his ponytail again.

He pulled back the blankets and tossed her onto the bed, then stripped away her sweats most efficiently, leaving her naked on the sheets. Leaning over her menacingly, he braced on his palms, sending an erotic shiver through her. "You know what happens to brats?"

"What?" she asked, heat rushing through her.

The rest of his face didn't change, just his eyes. He could say so much with those bourbon-brown beauties. "They get spanked."

Oh. He was serious. In the past, they'd experimented with bondage and blindfolding—but never discipline. Except perhaps one time when he refused to let her come, torturing her by keeping her on the edge, delaying her orgasm.

But this? This was new.

He captured her lips for a quick kiss before saying, "I've noticed what e-books you've been reading."

"Y-you're spying on me?" she asked, almost choking on the words.

"We have a family subscription to your e-book service. Whenever you download a book, I receive a message that the same title is available to me to read. I would hardly call that spying."

Her face felt as if she'd put it in an oven. She couldn't imagine what he thought of some of her smutty choices. Although they'd been lovers for eight months, she was still discovering what she liked, and had read a wide range of romantic erotica to get ideas about what she might try.

Apparently, so had Henry. And just because she'd bought a complete series of domestic discipline books recently didn't mean she was interested in a very personal demonstration.

Or was she?

"Do you remember your safe word?" he asked, his voice low and growly and threatening.

Pleasure curled in her belly at the sound. She'd read about spankings and wondered but had hesitated to suggest adding them to the mix, even though she'd felt a thrill reading about them.

It seemed she was about to learn if the real deal was as sexy as the fantasy.

"My safe word is Anne-Louise."

He growled when she said the name. But that was the safe word he'd given her—guaranteed to stop him from doing anything he found pleasurable.

Then, still holding her gaze, he peeled his t-shirt over his head. She could tell by the way he tightened his abs, the way he posed, the way he grinned seductively, that he was peacocking. Not to mention the full erection straining against his sweatpants. His desire stroked her through the crystal, coiling tight between her legs, and the rush of blood left her slickly wet. And yet they'd hardly touched.

His posing reminded her of a pirate hero. The way he'd thrown her over his shoulder earlier, and now the way he flexed his muscles. She could easily imagine him in close-fitting black pants, a flowing, see-through linen shirt, and a big silk sash tied around his waist, with a tricorn hat tilted cockily on his head.

Now there's a fantasy we could indulge in. Maybe next year's Halloween costume—

He *whooshed*, rolling her across his knee and running his hand over her naked bottom, which he gave a spank.

"Hey!" A harsher sting played out against the sensitive skin now that clothing no longer protected her bottom from his palm. A tingle ran between her legs again, too.

He cupped her breast, gliding his thumb over her nipple. "You allowed your mind to wander away from me."

"I was picturing you in a swashbuckler's costume."

He chuckled deeply, and his other hand caressed her butt cheek, soothing the sting. "Well, in that case, you are forgiven—for your lack of attention. But not for pulling my ponytail. Three times. And for saying I brood. For those offenses, you will be punished."

Before she could argue, he spanked one cheek, then the other, alternating four times; the sharp smacks filled the room.

Goddess, she hoped Rolf and Karen couldn't hear the sound.

The sting radiated across her skin, meeting the tingle between her legs, merging into one. She squirmed, feeling his rock-hard erection pressed against her side and his belly. He was enjoying this as much as she was.

Warmth surged through her, excitement and fear intermingling. She knew she had the power to tease him into doing *this*, but now, over his lap, she was powerless.

"Cerissa?" *Smack*. "Do you want to use your safe word?"

Well, maybe not completely powerless.

"No, sir." She'd read enough to recite the proper way to answer.

"Good girl."

Apparently she wasn't the only one who knew the proper reply.

Smack.

She squirmed again. The coil in her lower belly tightened, but the repeated spanks burned, sending too much sensation to her heated flesh.

He rubbed his hand over her butt again, the cool, smooth feeling a counterpoint to the sting.

Smack.

That last one caught her off guard, and she squealed.

"Will you behave yourself now?"

"I'll be good, I promise."

"Yes, you will," he said in that dark, masculine way that shot right to her core.

With her still facedown in his lap, he dipped two fingers between her legs, pressing into her, sliding easily inside. When he pulled them out, she moaned over the loss, but then they circled her clit repeatedly, spreading her slick arousal, and she almost exploded.

He rolled her onto her back, dangling her legs over the side of the bed, and untied his sweatpants, letting them drop to ruck around his ankles. He didn't even bother to kick them off. Without a word, he kneed her thighs apart, hooked his hands under her knees, raising her, and, with a roguish smile, thrust deep inside.

Oh my Goddess.

Having her legs raised pressed the heat of her reddened bottom harder against the bed, lighting her punished skin on fire. Erotic excitement sparked through her at his sudden, deep thrust.

He slid his hands along her calves, placed her heels on the mattress's edge, then took her wrists in his hands, holding them at her side. His tongue scraped over his fangs as he met her gaze.

Goddess, did he look dangerous—and darkly hot.

Curving his back to reach her nipples, he sucked and tongued them. She had no chance to resist, and she didn't want to. The rough thrusts had her moaning for more as his tongue hardened her nipples into tight buds.

She pressed her heels against the mattress's edge, rising to meet him, thrust for thrust, feeling the sensation flowing from her nipples to her clit. The way he filled her, the way he rubbed her, the way he teased her, both delighted and taunted her.

Through the crystal, his love flowed, but she could still feel the edge of his anger driving him faster, rougher, winding the spring deep within her until it was almost ready to snap.

His fangs brushed the sensitive flesh around her nipple, and the anticipation drove her crazy.

Biting there would hurt, but a good hurt.

"Cerissa?" he growled against her nipple.

"Yes, please."

He bit. A slight, sharp pain and then pure fire filled her veins. His mouth sucked her harder and his cock pounded into her, and she teetered on the edge, closer and closer. Then he angled his hips just a touch more, grinding against her clit. Still gripping each of her wrists, he pinned them near her shoulders.

Struggling to resist the restraint dropped her over that steep precipice.

She arched her back, fell, and shattered. Riding wave after wave of ecstasy, she was barely aware when he shuddered with his own orgasm until he at last thrust so hard and deep that she felt she'd come again.

He continued lapping at the areole of her breast, keeping the blood from dripping. Her nerves were so overstimulated, she'd scream if he touched her nipples again. When the bite stopped bleeding on its own, he planted another kiss on the mound and rose to see her, pinning her wrists by her ears.

Wow. She'd liked the beast in bed. A lot.

"Hi," she said breathlessly.

His erection still firmly inside her, he loomed over her, concern on his face. "Are you all right?"

"I'm fine, Quique. Very fine."

"Yes, you are." He averted his eyes, a guilty expression replacing his concern. "I shouldn't have spanked you. I shouldn't vent my anger on you. I—"

She shook his hand off her wrist and pressed a finger against his lips. "I knew what I was doing when I pulled your ponytail. I thought it might help with whatever's been bothering you. Besides, we've tried other things. I was curious about this one, as you so embarrassingly pointed out."

"So, you provoked me on purpose?"

She blushed. "Perhaps."

He chuckled. "And now that your curiosity has been satisfied?"

"Just like tickling—we might include a very occasional spanking in our rotation of fun."

He leaned in close to her lips, and his hot breath caressed her skin. "In that case, if you ever pull my ponytail again, I'll show you what a real spanking feels like."

Goddess, that made her hot all over again. She clenched around his waning erection, and it came to life inside her.

The kiss that followed confirmed what she sensed through the crystal. The anger had drained from him as he filled her, leaving behind only the deep love they felt for each other.

Chapter 14

CHALLENGE

**INDEPENDENCE MOUNTAIN BACK COUNTRY—THE NEXT
NIGHT**

The full moon illuminated the mountainside, making the landscape below Henry visible in minute detail. Standing by the helicopter's open door, the wind whipping stray strands of hair from underneath his helmet, he took in the vast wilderness that was his to conquer. Exhilaration raced through him. Nothing would stop him from the thrill of crushing the ungroomed, pristine slopes.

He'd felt better after making love to Cerissa, but Anne-Louise's annoying tug still came regularly enough to stir his anger again. Tonight he'd exorcise his demons on the mountain rather than in the bedroom.

As much as he'd enjoyed seeing Cerissa's pretty bottom turn pink, guilt plagued him over playing so roughly with her, even though she hadn't seemed to mind. In fact, she'd even suggested they include occasional rough play in their future repertoire.

A smile quirked his lips. She was the only person to have the audacity to yank on his ponytail. Everyone else—all prior girlfriends—had been warned off by his dark, forbidding glances. Not Cerissa.

Then he considered some of their other sexual adventures. No matter how smart and self-actualized his beautiful mate was, sometimes she enjoyed obeying him in bed.

He couldn't say that completely surprised him.

After making love, he'd held her as she slept. The rhythm of her heart was a meditation metronome that allowed him to ignore Anne-Louise's annoying pull. Finally, sunrise in New York put an end to his maker's call and gave him a few hours of peace before it was time for him to sleep. He'd even followed Father Matt's previous advice and journaled about his irritation and anger. There'd be plenty of fodder for confession when he returned to the Hill.

Tonight, the tug had resumed at dusk, and he couldn't wait to hit the slopes. The challenge would surely draw his focus away from his maker's demands and relieve some of the stress riding him.

The helicopter pilot, Roger Lee, knew all the best places for big mountain skiing. The vampire and his mortal partner, June, regularly flew extreme skiers into the back country. The couple dropped them off in the powder at the top so they could ski over pristine terrain to the base of the mountain. Henry had met the couple on prior trips and was pleased Rolf made the arrangements to use their service again.

Because of a minor storm that started earlier in the afternoon, they couldn't get airborne until after it died down. They arrived at the bowl's top ridge after midnight. The helicopter hovered for the drop-off above the tree line. Rolf went first, sitting on the edge of the cabin doorway with his skis on. He pushed off and landed on the fresh powder.

Henry double-checked he'd fastened the chin strap to his helmet, then followed closely behind his friend. Once on the slope, they waved the chopper off. As planned, Rolf led the way for the first half of their journey. Something about being in the open, a clear night sky over them, a ton of powder below, and only a few pine trees in sight, fostered a sense of peace within him. He loved the experience, loved being outdoors. His only regret was that Cerissa wasn't there to share it with him.

At a third of the way down the steep ridge, a low engine roar hit his ears, and his opinion abruptly flipped—he was grateful Cerissa hadn't accompanied them.

Somewhere on the mountain, an avalanche had started.

The low roar gradually grew louder, then closer, like a massive plane bore down on them. Rolf cut sideways across the slope, trying to dodge its path.

Snow and rocks plunged past Henry, then the full force hit him from behind. He tried riding the top of it, a surfer going for the upper curl of the wave, but the undertow pulled him below. He plummeted, tumbling as his skis popped off from the fury of the fall. Then his arm caught on something, and agony ripped through him, a pain he'd never felt before, so sharp, so excruciating, his brain couldn't process the torture.

When he came back to consciousness, it was still dark. He didn't know where Rolf was, he didn't know where he was, but he knew one thing: the avalanche had left him catastrophically injured.

Black Bear Restaurant and Bar—Around the same time

The log-cabin-style restaurant was warm and cozy with a fireplace at one end, a fire blazing within it, and a bartender staffing a full bar on the other end. Dining tables were scattered throughout the enormous room under an open-beamed ceiling.

The deep rumble reached Cerissa, where she sat next to the fireplace, drinking hot chocolate with Karen, having finished a late dinner.

Her hypersensitive hearing deciphered the sound before anyone else in the room, and she froze in her chair.

A moment later, Karen blanched white. "Avalanche."

The bartender switched the house television from sports to the local emergency broadcast channel. Early reports confirmed that an avalanche occurred close to the ridge where their mates skied.

Cerissa phoned Roger Lee's base camp. "Where are Henry and Rolf?"

"On the mountain. I dropped them off over twenty minutes ago. They were skiing when the slide started. Do you want me to alert the authorities?"

Cerissa glanced at Karen, who gripped the chair arms so hard, her fingers paled even whiter. "I'll call you again shortly. Don't do anything until I phone you." She threw cash on the table to cover their meals and grabbed Karen by the arm. "We need to leave. I can't help from here."

The direct order seemed to calm Karen's panic and bring her back to the present. Halfway past the door, something ripped through Cerissa's heart, a pain so intense she lost her breath. Clutching a hand to her chest, she collapsed onto a bench by the valet.

"What's wrong?" Karen asked.

"I don't know. Get the SUV. Hurry."

Karen rushed to the valet and handed him the ticket. When he returned with their car, they sped back to the condo.

Cerissa ran inside and changed into her ski suit and snowshoes—both designed for freezing temperatures and icy surfaces so she could traverse the rough terrain. In human form, hypothermia could incapacitate her. Although it wouldn't kill her, she would be useless to the guys without cold weather protection. While dressing, she explained to Karen what she was going to do.

They didn't have the option of calling the mortal authorities for a search and rescue, not this late in the night. If a mortal rescue party unearthed them after sunrise, the consequences would be disastrous. With any luck, Henry and Rolf would burrow under the snow during the day, and then escape the next night. Her fear: the avalanche had left them on the surface, exposed, and too injured to dig down to create a safe spot to hide in. If that happened, the rising sun would kill them.

The crystal's connection between her and Henry had cut off. Just as the pain ripped through her chest and subsided, she lost all sense of his emotions. None remained. At all.

Was he suppressing the crystal's connection? Or had he been knocked unconscious? Or even worse—

She wouldn't let her wild imaginings go there, couldn't contemplate losing him.

Instead, she suppressed her own panic and didn't voice any concerns, because if she did, the fear might paralyze her.

After gearing up, she hugged her bestie. "Stay here. Keep an eye on Bear. I'll call you within the hour."

Cerissa stepped away and thought, *Take me to him.*

The crystal embedded in his wrist transported her to it, and she materialized on top of a deep snow pile. His gloved hand was buried at least a yard from her grasp.

She dug into the snow, creating a tunnel between herself and his fingertips. Once she touched them, she wiggled a little more, wrapped her hand firmly around his, and pulled.

She'd expected to use his dead weight as leverage to move her closer to him. Instead, his hand slid to her with no resistance. It was then she realized the problem. His left hand and forearm ending at the elbow joint were no longer attached to his body. The fear and shock gurgled up her throat and she screamed, "Henry!"

INDEPENDENCE MOUNTAIN BACK COUNTRY—AROUND THE SAME TIME

Snow covered Henry. Pushing with the only hand he had left, rolling his body side to side and thumping his helmeted head to compress the snow above him, he enlarged the space entrapping him.

"Rolf, can you hear me?" he yelled.

"Over here. I can't move."

"Keep talking."

Zeroing in on the sound of his friend's voice, Henry gritted his teeth against the pain but burrowed toward Rolf. He dug with his right hand and dragged his injured left arm beside him, leaving a glistening trail of blood.

The snow, loosened by the avalanche, was rife with air pockets, and he made the most of them to inch forward.

From the limited amount of moonlight penetrating the snowpack, he guessed they were under about ten feet of powder and debris, if not more. Running out of oxygen wasn't a problem for them, and they could always tunnel to the top and hike to civilization.

Unless they were too wounded to do so.

When he reached Rolf, Henry pushed the snow aside, compacting it to make a small cavern where he could partially sit upright with his back curled. "How are you, my friend?"

Rolf stayed prone, stretched on his back, and cradled his wrist. "My left leg is broken, and I think my right arm is as well." Both wounds would heal with time, but it meant they weren't going anywhere tonight. "What about you?"

"A passing tree asked for a handout." Henry rolled his ski jacket's cuff and displayed his wounded elbow joint where his forearm was missing. His white turtleneck sleeve was stained red as the blood dripped from the raw tissue.

Rolf grimaced. "*Ach.* That is the worst joke you've ever told. I was going to suggest you hike to the ridge's base and come back for me tomorrow night."

"Aside from the fact I would not leave you here alone, I am losing too much blood to make the trip. But you should take advantage of it. One of us needs to heal quickly."

Henry held his severed artery over Rolf's mouth. The curative properties of his blood would mend the broken bones faster. "Do you have your phone?"

Rolf latched his lips to the open wound and, with his functioning hand, searched his belt. "Gone," he said with a gurgle as he swallowed.

"That is unfortunate, given mine is somewhere underneath the Santiago Express lift. But even if we had one, it's unlikely we'd get a signal out."

Rolf mumbled his agreement, working his throat to swallow the healing liquid he'd sucked from Henry's arm.

Henry fumbled around his jacket pocket and retrieved two small pouches. They'd survived the crash unopened. Still holding his wounded arm over Rolf's mouth, Henry bit the cap off one and squeezed the contents onto his own tongue, gulping it down.

Blood continued to drip from his elbow joint into Rolf's mouth, who swallowed without closing his lips. "What was in that pouch? Another concoction your mate made?"

Henry flushed with sexual energy, dampened somewhat by the pain he was in, but the contents instantly amped his own healing. "A concentrated form of mortal blood. Almost no plasma, mostly red blood cells. I have one here for you, but I must warn you, the side effects are disconcerting until you grow accustomed to the feeling."

After his experience in New York, when he and Tig tracked the Carlyle Cutter all night, he swore never to be trapped without dark wine again. So he'd started carrying the small pouches.

The skin where Henry's forearm was severed scabbed over. Since the bleeding stopped, he lowered his arm.

Rolf tried to move his leg. "Argh," he bellowed, flinching.

"Patience. It'll take time to heal. Let me examine the extent of your damage." Henry probed Rolf's injured arm with his right hand. From what his fingertips told him, it wasn't a bad break. A hairline fracture would likely heal during the day, particularly with the healing boost Henry's own blood provided.

Rolf's leg, on the other hand, had a compound fracture poking through the ripped pant leg. Henry pushed back more snow to increase the space above the injured leg so he could work. It would heal faster if he reset the bones. With Rolf's help, they opened a pocketknife, and Henry sliced a bigger opening in the stretchy black ski pants.

The skin split where the splintered tibia jutted above the top of his ski boot's hard shell, and trails of blood flowed over and dotted the snow.

"Hold on." Henry would never attempt this with a mortal. It was too dangerous for them. It could send them into shock and fail to set the bones properly. But immediate first aid for a vampire prevented the bone fragments from healing in the wrong place. The leg wouldn't have to be broken and reset again.

Using his own feet to hook around Rolf's ski boot and applying leverage, Henry wrapped his uninjured arm around the knee to pull the bone fragments together carefully. He tucked the ends within the skin and butted them against each other so they interlaced like two puzzle pieces. He then used what remained of his upper arm to press the bones back into alignment. Wrapping his belt around the break and pulling snugly stabilized the bones in place.

Rolf had made no sound during the procedure.

Ever the stoic.

Then Henry focused on his friend's face and realized Rolf had passed out.

Between resetting the bones plus the vampire blood Henry had donated, Rolf's leg should heal enough to allow him to hike through the wilderness at sunset.

But Henry's arm? That was another matter entirely.

CHAPTER 15

FRIGHTENING VISION

MOUNTAIN TOP CONDOS—AROUND THE SAME TIME

With Henry's hand in hers, Cerissa flashed back to the condo.

Karen screamed.

"Easy. It's Henry's." Cerissa shoved the amputated forearm behind her, her mind scrambling like Bear's toenails on the tile floor—which he was doing at that very minute, yipping and trying to grab the severed limb from her.

To hide the appendage, she stuffed it in the refrigerator and pushed Bear away to close the door, then joined Karen on the couch. "But I didn't find anything else—they're probably trapped under the snow. I tried phoning him but didn't hear any ringing."

Leaning over, Karen had her face between her knees, panting. She looked as if she might faint. "That part of the mountain, they won't have any signal bars. But even if they did, Henry doesn't have his phone."

Cerissa rubbed Karen's back. "Why wouldn't he?"

"Rolf told me Henry smashed it against the rocks last night while they were on the ski lift, after receiving a call from Marcus. Henry didn't want you to know he lost control of his temper."

Yeah, she got that. He felt ashamed. But he was withholding more from her than a pique of anger. Marcus's call must have delivered bad news. Not that it mattered right now.

"The replacement phone was supposed to arrive today but didn't." Karen sat up and chewed on a fingernail, rocking herself. "I can't think what to do."

Cerissa called Roger. She couldn't tell him what she'd found or how she found it, but she could tell him a white lie—that the loyalty bond between her and Henry seemed to be broken, which alerted him to the severity of the situation. "Are there any other vampires on the mountain who could mount a rescue operation?"

"Nah. Just me and the wife. There isn't much night work, and it's hard to get fresh blood up here without preying on the tourists, which isn't good for business."

"Can you search for them?"

"Not tonight. Can't put the chopper in the air—the wind's kicked up again."

She thanked him and tapped the disconnect button. With no other options, she'd have to go hunting herself.

"Can't you track him using your Lux tech?" Karen asked.

"Our flash technology can track my blood in his body, except it's been over twenty-four hours since he last drank from me, and he only took light sips." She stared at the app on her phone. "I can't get a lock on it. Also, he doesn't have his phone, and I haven't put a tracking app on Rolf's."

She explained part of her plan to Karen—the part Karen would play—as she crammed supplies into a backpack, then dashed into the bathroom, disrobed, and wrapped a towel around her naked body. The empty contact lens case on the vanity reminded her. Should she remove her contact lenses? They gave her some advantages, but she hated the way they felt on animal eyeballs.

Not worth it.

They'd just be a distraction. When she triggered the ejection process, small, tentacle-like threads retracted, disconnecting from her optic nerve. She shuddered at the slight shock and popped the lenses into a spare case.

Ready, she returned to the living room to say goodbye to Karen, set the flash disk on a thirty-second delay to transport her, zipped it into the backpack pouch, and morphed into a timber wolf. The towel fell to the floor. Bear lunged toward Cerissa's wolf and whined when Karen held the poor puppy back by his harness.

Wearing only the backpack, Cerissa shook her fur, waited for the program to trigger itself, and then flashed to where she'd found Henry's forearm. She sniffed at the snow, caught his scent, and howled into the night.

The hunt began.

INDEPENDENCE MOUNTAIN BACK COUNTRY—AROUND THE SAME TIME

Henry chewed on ice crystals. Hunger clawed at him—the injury drove his body's craving for mortal blood—but water would help a little with his thirst. Rolf woke about an hour later.

"How are you doing?" Henry asked.

"My leg is on fire and my arm hurts like a son of a bitch. Aside from that, fine."

"I have the other pouch for you. Do you want it now?"

"Yes, I'm starving. I need to feed if I'm going to climb down the ridge tomorrow night."

"I must warn you again. The side effects can be overwhelming." Henry broke the plastic cap off and placed the mini-pouch in Rolf's left hand. Rolf lifted it to his mouth and sucked it dry.

"*Ach mein Gött!*" he exclaimed.

Cerissa had once described the concentrated form of blood as "Viagra for vampires."

"I warned you." Henry waited as his friend fought against the effects. "I am going to tunnel to the outside."

Without waiting for an answer, Henry began the arduous task of digging out with one hand. He burrowed upward at a slant, so he'd have an easier time closing the top end before the sun rose. It took longer than he assumed it would. By the time he located the surface, the pinkish shades of dawn peeked above the mountain range.

He didn't have his daylight bracelet with him, and ducked underground.

It was then that he heard the howl of a wolf. He yelled, and the wolf howled back. It had to be Cerissa. But he couldn't wait for her; he couldn't fall asleep in the open when night ended. Slipping off his neck gaiter, he rubbed it across his forehead to transfer his scent. Afterward, he struggled to tie the gaiter one-handed to a nearby stick and plant his flag at the opening of the tunnel.

Then he shoveled snow to cover the hole and block the light, and made the return journey, crawling backward toward their cavern. So long as he and Rolf were at least eighteen inches from the surface, the sunlight wouldn't penetrate and burn them. Rolf waited more than ten feet below in the small chamber their bodies had created. They'd both be safe there.

By the time he crawled to the bottom of the slanting tunnel, Henry's internal clock told him sunrise was imminent. He could feel the tug of sleep overtaking him. Rolf had passed out already.

Henry checked to make sure that no part of Rolf's skin was exposed. Even at this depth, it wasn't worth the risk. Ski gear concealed just about every inch of him. Henry removed a survival blanket out of Rolf's jacket pocket, struggled one-handed to unfold the small rectangle into a flat sheet, and covered Rolf from his face to his feet. Whatever weak amount of sunlight might penetrate the snow would bounce off the Mylar blanket. Henry then took a similar one out of his own jacket pocket, unfolded it with much frustrated effort, and lay back, covering himself, before falling asleep.

Independence Mountain back country—Sunrise

Cerissa sniffed at the neck gaiter. Her sensitive nose confirmed the owner: *Henry*. She'd arrived moments too late to flash them away before daylight hit, and howled her frustration. But the flag was a reassuring sign, and she could see the slanted tunnel below the rocks and snow. The guys must have tunneled to a sufficient depth to be safe.

Although she considered digging to where they were and flashing them to a lightproof room in the condo, she couldn't take the risk of exposing them to the sun. Opening the tunnel might very well do just that, and she hadn't brought a daylight bracelet with her. But even if she went back to the condo to retrieve a bracelet, returned, and dug down, sunlight might reach them through the tunnel before she could get both of them under the protection cast by the bracelet.

No, she couldn't uncover them safely. She'd have to wait until tonight.

And she couldn't flash herself beneath the snow, either. She needed to materialize in an area big enough for her body that was empty of any solid matter. The ice crystals were too much of an impediment.

With her teeth, she loosened the backpack she wore, wiggled out of its straps, and dropped it by the gaiter flag. The backpack held six pouches of self-heating blood. As soon as they woke and dug to the surface, the guys could feed.

It also contained the only flash disk she owned, along with her phone. Her plan: if Henry phoned Karen's number, Cerissa could then provide instructions and talk him through using the flash disk. She'd left the condo in such a hurry that she hadn't explained that part of the plan to Karen.

Or should she flash to the condo and come back tonight? She'd transferred the disk from her watch to a contact lens case so Henry could access and tap it. Direct contact with the disk was required to work it. Her watch crystal employed face-recognition software to swing it open and wouldn't recognize him.

She'd been so upset by finding Henry's arm, and was in such a rush to return to search for him, she'd neglected to add protective clothing to the backpack. Morphing from wolf to human would leave her naked in the freezing air while she removed the case.

What if her shivering fingers dropped the small, thin disk and she lost it in the snow? Then Henry wouldn't have it when he woke.

No. It was simpler to descend in wolf form and meet Karen, even if it wasn't a well-thought-out plan. Besides, once they rendezvoused and phoned Ari, he could use her phone as a tracking device and flash her back here to retrieve the guys. That was her backup idea if they were too injured to work their way to the surface.

She started the long trek down the ridge's steep slope. The sun had warmed the top layer, making the snow soft and loose under her paws, and with each step, she sank to her armpits—all four of them—then tried a sort of hopping stride, but that didn't make it any easier. She finally resigned herself to the fact it would take her all morning to arrive at the rendezvous point near Roger's base camp and meet Karen.

When she took another jump, Cerissa's front paws landed together, and something went *crack*. A thin dome of snow broke, and she scrambled for purchase, losing the battle, falling to land on the sharp rocks below her.

She woke at the bottom of a canyon, every part of her hurting. A deep slash across one paw ran further along her leg, and bloody prints remained behind as she limped away. Glancing around, she guessed she'd fallen into a huge ravine covered by a crust of powdery debris from the avalanche, which had created a snow dome. Water dripped onto her back as weak sunlight melted the ice above. Her limp grew worse. She accepted defeat and stopped trying to navigate the icy rocks.

Morphing to human, naked on the snow, she shivered and transformed back to wolf form, fully healing her paw and covering her body once again in warm, thick fur.

Hunger racked her belly. Three morphs in a short time period had left her weakened. She should have brought raw meat along as a pick-me-up snack, but she'd been so focused on Henry's needs, she forgot about her own.

She wasn't sure where the gully would lead, but she didn't trust herself to climb the sides of the icy cavern—the snow was too loose, her paw placements too uncertain. She might trigger another local slide or cause the top dome to come caving down on her.

So she followed the center culvert and hoped to make it off the mountain before nightfall.

CHAPTER 16

THE TREK

INDEPENDENCE MOUNTAIN BACK COUNTRY—THAT NIGHT

Henry woke at dusk and checked the access tunnel—it hadn't collapsed during the day, for which he said a brief prayer of gratitude. The pain in his savaged elbow had died down to a minor throb while he slept. Still, he struggled to shimmy up the tunnel one-handed, pushing the snow to the side and packing it in place. He braced with his remaining upper arm, using his helmet as a plow to make more room, until finally he cleared away the last few feet of snow at the top. When he made it to the surface, he discovered the backpack Cerissa had left behind.

Relief coursed through him—both because she'd found them, and because it meant she hadn't spent the day worrying. He struggled to open the backpack and spotted six self-warming pouches. He squeezed one, shakily peeled the plastic wrapper off the straw, and tried to insert the straw one-handed. The sharp point of the straw kept sliding off instead of piercing the pouch. His position wasn't helping—sitting on the tunnel's top ledge with his legs dangling into the hole. So he propped the pouch between his knees and finally pierced the foil seal. Much to his irritation, a few drops escaped at the straw's base to roll down and stain his ski pants. He then latched his lips on to the straw and sucked the life-giving sustenance in big gulps.

When Rolf emerged from the tunnel, Henry passed over a pouch. "Cerissa found us."

"Where is she?"

"I don't know. She wasn't here when I crawled out. But those are her tracks." Henry pointed to a series of paw prints in the snow. "We should follow them. How is your arm?"

"Mostly healed." Rolf prepped his own pouch and drained it quickly. "Is there anything else in the bag?"

"More dark wine and a phone. But I cannot get a signal yet." They each drank a second pint, and Henry put the empties into the backpack and slipped it on his back.

Even Anne-Louise's nudging didn't bother him, surrounded as he was by the relaxing, crisp smell of wet pine trees and the burgeoning hope they'd make it off the mountain relatively unscathed. His breath swirled to form foggy ice crystals in the air. The clear night sky, a canopy of bright dots above him, and the pleasant prospect of soon arriving at the warm condo and seeing Cerissa again, helped his mood as well. The situation could have been so much worse.

With a reluctant sigh, Henry prepared for the descent down the dangerous slope.

"How is your leg doing?" he asked.

"Not fully healed. I can't put weight on it."

Henry found a couple of good-sized sticks and, with Rolf's help, fashioned a splint. Using the blade of his pocketknife, he had Rolf cut the empty sleeve off his own cotton turtleneck shirt. They made strips of fabric and, together with both of their belts, tied the sticks around Rolf's leg to keep it straight. Although the bones had initially knitted during the day, the tibia would remain fragile for a while, and he didn't want the shinbone breaking again.

"We'll work together to make it to the base." Henry's elbow had regenerated during the night, but it would be more than a week before his hand regrew completely. He needed Rolf's help as much as Rolf needed his.

Henry offered his shoulder for Rolf to brace on, and his friend pushed with one leg to stand, then transferred weight onto the trussed leg. "I'm as ready as I'm going to be."

"Lean on me. You look unsteady still."

Henry slipped his uninjured arm around Rolf's waist, and Rolf draped his around Henry's shoulders. Following Cerissa's tracks, they hobbled down the mountain. At one point, they had to veer to avoid a cavern in the snow. After that, her paw prints disappeared, which bothered him. Where could she have gone? The road was downhill. If they kept hiking in that direction, they should reach it. But why hadn't Cerissa?

Halfway there, they stopped to consume one more pouch each of dark wine, grateful she'd packed the extra two. The pain in his amputated arm throbbed harder with exertion, and taking a rest break helped. As they resumed their trek, the pain returned, and when he spotted the road below them, relief cascaded through him.

He grabbed the phone Cerissa had left them and punched in Karen's number. This time the call went through.

"Cerissa? Is that you?" Karen asked anxiously.

"No, this is Henry."

"Oh, God, am I glad to hear your voice. Is Rolf with you? Is he okay?"

"Yes, to both questions. We are almost to the road. So Cerissa's not with you?"

"She went to find you using the crystal and located your arm instead. So she went back in wolf form and didn't return."

"She left us a backpack with dark wine pouches. We followed her trail for a bit and then lost the tracks. She must have come down another way."

"That doesn't make sense. She was going to leave the blood if she found you and meet me at Roger's base camp. Then she'd go back tonight to retrieve you. She didn't show up. I just assumed she'd slept with you guys."

"Please come get Rolf. I'm going to climb back up and find her. Load our largest backpack with the rappelling equipment we brought. And food. Power bars, meat, whatever is in the refrigerator. If she is up there and injured, she will need fuel to regenerate. Understand?"

"Yes. I should be in your vicinity within twenty-five minutes."

"You and Rolf share the loyalty bond, yes?"

"Sure—I can already feel the pull of him calling to me."

"Good. Follow that tug. Oh, and check the local news for reports of any wolf sightings. Unlikely, but animal control might have picked her up if she's been hurt."

"Got it. Will do."

"We will wait near the road. Goodbye."

Henry helped Rolf traverse the last bit of the slope's base. In places, they slid on their backsides rather than clambering down. "What are you planning to do?" Rolf asked as he pushed himself upright.

"I am going to go back and find her."

"You don't think she'll come off the mountain on her own?"

"If she could, she would have by now. Her plan was to climb down during the day, then come back for us. She didn't. That means she's in trouble."

When they reached the road, Karen waited with the engine running. She must have spotted them on the hillside and parked below. They were all lucky the authorities hadn't closed off access. Probably because the hefty v-ditch protecting the road had stopped the avalanche and the dammed-up snow didn't present a threat to traffic.

"Rolf!" Karen jumped out of the rental SUV and ran to her mate, throwing her arms around him.

"It's okay, *Liebling*, I'm fine," he whispered, stroking her hair and patting her back. "Let's get in the car where it's warm." He leaned on her as he hobbled to the SUV.

"Are you hurt?"

"My leg broke, but it's healing." He climbed into the front seat with Henry's help.

"Any word on wolf sightings?" During their journey, the question had bothered him. How could he assert ownership over a wild wolf found by animal control? He shook it off. If necessary, he'd steal her from them.

Karen's gaze locked on his bloody coat sleeve, and her face paled, then she covered her mouth, making a gagging noise.

Was she about to throw up? He hoped not, and turned his left side away from her so she couldn't focus on his injury.

"How did it happen?" she asked, her voice rough.

"Ripped off by a tree. It's unimportant. Any word of an injured wolf?"

"Ah, none." She swallowed so hard her throat bobbed. "I even called the parks and wildlife ranger station. They acted like I was some sort of loon."

Which meant Cerissa was still on the mountain.

Henry got in the back seat and grabbed the backpack Karen had brought. He ripped the one he wore off his shoulders and tossed it aside, before slipping Cerissa's phone into a zippered pocket of his ski jacket. He'd use the larger backpack instead of the small one Cerissa left behind. It would hold more gear.

"Why didn't she flash back to the condo? Doesn't she have her watch with her?"

Karen shrugged. "I assume she does. She was in such a rush; she didn't tell me that part of her plan."

Reaching over the seat back into the cargo area, he added rope, carabiners, and a rappelling harness to the backpack, taking them from the equipment box. He leaned forward and popped the spring latches on the stiff plastic ski boots, removed them from his feet, and pulled on the thick-soled snow boots Karen had remembered to bring.

As he worked at vampire speed to get ready, worry over Cerissa's well-being propelled him. Karen took the driver's seat and again threw her arms around Rolf, who removed his padded gloves and put his hands in front of the heater vents.

"Henry," Karen said, "there are snowshoes for you too, to go over your boots, and I threw in some of the ice-climbing equipment, too."

"Excellent planning. It may come in handy." Henry handed Rolf another pouch of blood then drank one himself before adding two more to the backpack. If he had to spend the night searching for Cerissa, at least he would have sufficient sustenance. "I'll climb to where we lost her tracks. If I don't find her, I'll dig under before sunrise. If I don't call by tomorrow night, send a search party for us."

Rolf cleared his throat. "Karen will, as I'm going with you."

"I appreciate the offer, but your broken leg will only hinder you. I can make better time on my own."

"Henry, you shouldn't go back on the mountain without me. You're injured. The snow is unstable. You could get trapped there, unable to hide from daylight."

"I thank you for your concern. But I will go alone."

Rolf grumbled. "If that foolish mate of yours had not stuck her nose where it didn't belong..."

"Enough. She tried to help us."

"We didn't need her help. Leave her up there. She'll find her way down, eventually."

"You know I can't do that."

Rolf swung around in his seat to face Henry. "Yes, you can. You conveniently forget what she really is. Let her people get her off that mountain if she's in trouble."

"You are fortunate she didn't think the same way when she saved Karen's life."

"I appreciate what she did for Karen. But that doesn't mean you have to risk your life right now. You have Cerissa's phone—call Ari to rescue her."

As harsh as he sounded, Rolf defaulted to expressing anger rather than fear. And he feared letting Henry go alone.

Sometimes, Henry had to read between the lines.

After tapping the contact for Ari, Henry put it on speaker—he still had his helmet on, covering his ears. The call went straight to voicemail. "You know what to do," the recording said. "And if you don't, what century are you living in?"

"Ari, this is Henry. I'm calling on Cerissa's phone. Mine has been...lost. Call Cerissa's phone or Karen's as soon as you receive this. Cerissa is missing, and we need your help to find her." Once he disconnected, he returned the phone to his zippered pocket.

He glanced to where his friends sat in the front seat, worry filling their eyes. "It's after sunset in California. Ari probably has his phone on refusal because Gaea just woke. Keep trying to reach him. I'm going after Cerissa. Now."

"You can't—"

"I can." Henry ignored Rolf and examined the gear in the backpack. He wasn't arguing any further. She wouldn't be in danger now if he hadn't dismissed her initial concern and insisted it was perfectly safe to indulge in a high-risk sport. She'd trusted him, but he hadn't considered how much his life had now evolved. In the past, he didn't have a romantic partner who cared if he lived or died, who would endanger themselves to rescue him, and who *could* help him in ways a mortal mate could not. Now he did.

It changed everything.

"I have all I need to climb the mountain. I'll keep Cerissa's phone. When we're ready to be picked up, I'll call."

Henry left the warm car, zipped his parka, and pulled the hood over his helmet and around his face. He slid his boots into the snowshoe toe boxes, then strapped on each one. Unlike the snowshoe of yesteryear, which resembled a small tennis racket, these were streamlined, with crampons on the soles for gripping ice and built-in mechanics to support flexing his foot.

It had taken him and Rolf about an hour and a half to make the trek, and would take longer for the hard ascent. At least they'd created a trail any amateur could follow. Now recharged with blood, he could use his enhanced vampire agility and strength to scale the slope, even though the exertion increased the throbbing in his arm.

When he arrived at the place where her paw prints ended, the chasm appeared bottomless despite his enhanced night vision. He struggled into the rappelling harness, hampered by his injury, but managed to attach the belay device, and fed rope through the locking carabiner. Then he wrapped the rope around a nearby tree and slung the snowshoes over his back. Being careful to avoid swinging and bumping the crusty opening's fragile edge, he fed the rope one-handed. The cavern plunged about sixty feet. Peering over his shoulder as he rappelled, he glimpsed blood on the rocks below him and inhaled a deep breath.

Fresh blood. Is it Cerissa's?

He let out the rope until his feet landed on broken rocks. He struggled to balance himself on the uneven surface, something he couldn't have done if he'd kept on the snowshoes. Once stable, he stuck a finger into the red ice crystals, brought it to his lips, and took a tentative taste to confirm—yes, it was Cerissa's, albeit in wolf form.

A trail of blood led off through the crevasse. Had she landed on the rocks and injured herself? He sniffed the cold air, seeking her scent, and followed the trail, which drew him much further east than the route he and Rolf had traversed.

The rocky culvert rose with the surrounding snow forming a lip, leveling off, and he scaled it to follow her tracks, then donned the snowshoes again. The blood trail disappeared at that point. She must have stopped bleeding. Tired and hurting, he continued to follow her paw prints.

Three hundred feet away, he spotted a brown mass against the white snow. His heart lurched as he climbed closer.

CHAPTER 17

TRAPPED

INDEPENDENCE MOUNTAIN—MOMENTS LATER

A wolf lay on the snow wounded—its leg crunched in an illegal leg-hold trap. A metal stake through a chain held the trap in place so the trap couldn't be dragged, leaving the animal no way to escape.

¡Por Dios! *Please let Cerissa be all right.*

Henry ran to the wolf, recognizing the scent of her, and dropped to his knees, listening for her heartbeat. Relief flooded him when he heard it. She appeared unconscious. Running his hands over her, checking for other damage, he found frozen blood matting the fur on her back leg, but she didn't have any other obvious injuries. "I'm here. Everything will be fine."

He stroked her head, and she opened her eyes, squinting and whining.

Using his foot to press one lever, he gripped the other with his right hand. His biceps shook as he fought against the springs, trying not to further hurt her. Muscle spasms sparked through his amputated arm as his whole body tensed. The rusted iron creaked, and finally the jagged jaws opened.

Freed, she whined again and crawled free.

Once she was clear, he let the jaws snap shut. If whoever owned the trap had been in front of him right then, he would have beaten them senseless.

She tried to stand but fell back onto her side. He rushed to her—either she didn't have the energy to morph and heal herself now, or hypothermia had set in. He shrugged off the backpack, rummaged for some dried meat, and attempted to feed her, but she wouldn't eat it.

Opening a bottle of water one-handed resulted in more liquid slopping onto the snow than remaining by the time he finished. He dribbled the remainder into her mouth, and she lapped it up.

Where was her flash disk? She wouldn't have put herself in jeopardy, wouldn't have gone searching without carrying one. She wasn't wearing her watch—not on either front leg or tied around her throat. Could she have affixed it to her fur? He ran his fingers through her ruff, in hopes he could find the transport device and flash them away. All he could figure was the fall knocked the disk loose, and she lost it in the snow.

No choice. He would have to carry her off the mountain. First, he discarded his helmet. The round polycarbonate outer shell would be too hard against her soft belly when he lifted her. Then he bent forward on his knees, his forehead pressed into the snow, and worked his way under her until she wrapped around his neck and lay over his shoulders. Carefully lifting her, he rose to his feet, and avoided touching her injured leg with his still-throbbing partial arm.

He tried to feed her as they descended. Propped on his shoulders, she nibbled on a little raw hamburger. Halfway down the mountain, she struggled to be released. He eased her off his shoulders and set her on the ground.

She was wobbly as she stood on three legs. He fed her more meat, which she gulped quickly, then took a step and collapsed. The leg was not healing on its own. He knelt next to her. "Do you want me to carry you?"

She gripped the strap of his backpack in her teeth and pulled on it.

"You want something in there?"

She licked his face, and he got the message. He shucked the backpack and opened it for her. She stuck her nose in and rooted around. Then she looked up at him, a question in her eyes.

What she wanted wasn't there.

"Are you looking for your backpack?" he asked her. She barked once in response. "I left it in the SUV."

She whined.

"What was in the backpack?"

With her nose, she put an imprint into the snow. A small circle.

"The flash disk. You placed it in the backpack for Rolf and me to use. I'm sorry, I didn't know."

She struggled to stand, only to collapse onto her side again.

"Don't try to walk. I'll carry you off the mountain."

He could hear the agony in her whine and found her medic kit—Karen had been smart enough to include the zippered case. Finding the jet injector, he dialed in a stabilizing hormone that would help with the pain while she maintained her wolf's shape until they reached the condo.

She must have agreed with his judgment, as she sat still and let him inject the medication.

After repacking and awkwardly hooking the backpack with his arms, he lifted her onto his shoulders again, despite his one-handed deficiency. She whined when he accidentally brushed the broken paw with his healed but tender elbow joint, and pain lanced through him with the contact.

"I'm sorry. It won't be much longer now."

He began the trek back down the slope, trudging away in the crunchy snow, trying to maintain his balance, and carrying her phone in his hand. When the screen showed enough signal bars, he punched in Karen's number. She answered immediately.

"I have Cerissa."

"Oh thank God," Karen replied.

"My guess—we'll come off the mountain a good half-mile further east from where you collected Rolf."

"I'm at the condo. I'll be there in twenty minutes at most."

"Load some blankets into the back seat. A lot of blankets. And towels. Anything to keep her warm."

They said goodbye. "We're almost there, *querida*."

Cerissa raised her muzzle and licked his face, and he let her. That was the most enthusiasm she'd shown since he rescued her.

When he arrived at the icy road, the SUV pulled up and the back hatch opened. Rolf leaned against the passenger door to steady himself as his feet hit the ground, and he hobbled to the rear of the SUV. "Let me help."

He braced his hip against the SUV's bumper and unwrapped Cerissa from Henry's shoulders. Moving carefully, he transferred her to the blankets in the cargo area.

"What's wrong with her? You do have the right wolf?"

"Yes, it's Cerissa." Henry covered her and then unfastened his snowshoes. "I don't know what's wrong. Possibly the injury, possibly the cold. Here, help me up."

With a steadying hand from Rolf, Henry crawled in next to her. He brushed the frozen snow off her head and muzzle with a towel.

"All in?" Rolf asked.

"Yes. Please get us back to the condo."

Rolf pressed the button to lower the hatch. He returned to the front seat, and Karen drove them down the winding roads that bordered the back-mountain wilderness.

"It is all right, *mi amor*," Henry whispered. "We will be there soon."

Cerissa's wolf form looked at him with deep brown eyes that held both pain and gratitude.

When they got to the condo, Henry asked Rolf to carry her inside. It was easier for him, with two hands, to lift her without hurting her further.

"Put her on the rug in front of the fireplace in her room." Henry hurried behind them, then lit the gas log, which *flumped* to life. Kneeling, he got on the floor with her.

Karen gnawed on a fingernail. "Is she going to be okay?"

"She'll be all right once she can morph. Please go to the kitchen and find something for her to eat." From the bathroom, Bear whined. "Rolf, if you could, please see to the puppy's needs?"

Rolf hobbled to the bathroom and had to carry the puppy. The dog struggled to get free to go to Cerissa's side.

"Once Bear has gone outside, bring him back. He can help keep her warm."

Karen returned to the bedroom with a package of deli-cut roast beef, already opened. That, combined with what she ate earlier, should be enough to let Cerissa morph.

"Karen, would you please gather some more dry blankets? I'll rewrap her after she morphs back into human form."

While Karen left to fetch the blankets, Henry fed Cerissa by hand. The wolf quickly gulped the soft meat.

Just as she finished eating, Karen hurried back with an armful of blankets, dumped them next to him, and petted Cerissa's head. "Come on, bestie. Come back to us."

"It's okay, *querida*." Henry massaged the wolf's withers. "You're safe."

Rolf returned with Bear off the leash, and the puppy raced to Cerissa and whined, licking her muzzle and cuddling against her belly. The puppy wouldn't settle, anxiously sniffing her before squirming again.

Henry didn't understand why she hadn't morphed. Then the answer came to him.

Cerissa was too modest to morph in front of the number of people in the room. But he didn't want to hurt Karen's feelings by bluntly saying so.

"Karen, perhaps it would help if you would heat some soup for her. The smell of food cooking might entice her back to human form. Rolf, why don't you go assist her?"

With a hand on Karen's back, Rolf ushered her out. "Come, *Liebling*."

After Rolf closed the door behind them, Henry planted a kiss on the top of his mate's head. "All right, Cerissa, we're alone. You can change back now."

He had barely spoken the words when she morphed.

"I'm so cold," was the first thing she said. He scooped her up, placed the dry blankets around her, and wrapped her in his arms. She pulled the puppy into her lap, and he curled up contentedly and stayed still for once.

Rubbing her hands felt like rubbing ice. He moved her closer to the fireplace. His body temperature was lower than most mortals, but at least he acted as an insulator. Between the blankets and the fire's heat, her skin slowly warmed.

A knock at the door. "Come in," Henry called.

Karen carried a large mug of soup and set it on the hearth. Cerissa could reach it if she wanted it. "It's good to see you back among us, girlfriend."

Rolf had followed and now stood in the doorway, watching.

"It-it's good to be back," Cerissa replied, her teeth chattering when she finished speaking.

"How is your leg?" Henry asked her.

"Ah, fine. I reconstructed it when I morphed."

Karen looked puzzled.

"An illegal trap broke her leg." An animal caught in the cruel jaws suffered a prolonged death from blood loss, dehydration, and hypothermia. Directing his next question to Cerissa, he asked, "Morphing doesn't help with the cold?"

"No." Her voice shook as she shivered. "T-the cold slows the molecules that comprise what I am, and they stay slow no matter what form I'm in. So while morphing can fix a broken bone, it doesn't cure the effects of h-hypothermia."

"You might feel better if you tried some of that soup." He brought the mug to her lips.

She wrapped her fingers over his, taking a sip. "That tastes wonderful." She sipped the broth until the mug emptied. "What else do we have to eat?"

He exhaled a sigh of relief. If she was hungry, she was on the way to mending. Karen went to raid the refrigerator again. Rolf pulled the door shut and left them alone.

Henry hugged Cerissa tightly and felt a shot of surprise when she loosened his arm to turn and kiss him.

"Thank you." She laid her head against his shoulder.

He held her, occasionally kissing the top of her head and thanking *Dios* she was all right.

"I'd like to put some clothes on, please."

He rose to his feet and rummaged through her luggage to find comfortable underwear, a pair of warm, soft pants and a long-sleeve t-shirt, and helped her to get dressed. She returned to the fireplace and snugged the blanket around herself. He sat next to her and took her in his arms. "Do you need anything else?"

"No, I'm slowly warming."

He held her for a few minutes with Bear on the floor using her leg as a pillow, snoozing already.

"I love you, Cerissa."

"I love you too, Henry. I was so afraid something had happened to you when the crystal cut off and I discovered your forearm."

"How did you find it?" he asked.

"The same way I would have found you. I focused on the crystal and asked it to bring me to you. By the way, your forearm is in the refrigerator."

Henry let out a surprised laugh. "Why on earth did you save it?"

Cerissa stroked his injured arm, wanting to ask a question, but not sure how he'd react. "I saved it because I didn't know if we could reattach it."

"Aha, I see. That isn't necessary. I'll grow a new one."

"Oh, that's a relief." She'd been afraid the amputation would be permanent. "Then, in that case, I'll remove the crystal from the severed limb. Once your arm grows back, we can implant it in your, ah, new wrist."

"Will it need to recalibrate to you again?"

"I doubt it, but I could check the Lux database to see if there have been any case histories. Losing a forearm isn't a common experience."

"Indeed."

"And you'll want to retrieve your watch. Your Patek Phillipe is still attached."

"Good to know." He chuckled lightly and hugged her again, pressing his partial arm against her back. She had yet to see the extent of the damage. Although, as a doctor, she was inured to the sight of grotesque trauma, the thought of seeing him injured made her cringe.

Still, she had to confirm he was all right. "May I examine it?"

Pulling back the jagged edge of his shirt sleeve, he showed her how the nub of his elbow had regenerated.

Not as bad as she first imagined. No sign of torn flesh or scabby wounds. The regrown skin smoothed over the joint. "It's been just over twenty-four hours and it's grown back this much already?"

"Yes. With sufficient blood, I heal from most injuries after one sleep. This will take a little longer—maybe a week."

She shivered.

"Do you need another blanket?"

"No, it's just—" She pivoted on her butt to face him, her back to the fireplace, her legs crossed. "I can't stop thinking that something worse could have happened to you. Are you in pain?"

"Mildly. Nothing that won't pass with time."

"Promise me you won't do anything foolhardy like this again."

H enry hugged her to his chest, holding her tight. "Cerissa, it was a fluke. I have heli-skied many times with no problem. But you are right. My life is different now that I have you as a true mate, now that we are getting married. I will not risk myself so greatly if it means risking you in your attempt to aid me again. I will aim to be more cautious going forward."

"Thank you. I don't want to be that afraid again."

"Neither do I." High-risk sports were one way he gave himself that shot of adrenaline to distract from stress so he'd feel alive. Maybe it was time to try something different for distraction, such as yoga.

He released her, and she looked at him, caution in her eyes. "And you need to get your anger under control, Quique. Your phone may have worked—if you had it on you."

"Ah, you found out what happened to my phone?"

"You threw it on the rocks after a call with Marcus, though I didn't learn why."

He huffed. Anger would always be the emotion he struggled with the most. "I will try to better control it. That is all I'll promise."

"I don't know what I'd do if I lost you." She hugged him tightly. "I was so scared when we first heard about the avalanche, and then again when I couldn't find you."

"*Mi amor*, I will never leave you." Never. He hadn't exchanged marriage vows with anyone before—he'd never loved another like he loved her. He'd do everything in his power to keep her forever. "But you, you must consider your own safety before rushing to my aid, *cariña*. You didn't do so last night. You must stop trying to rescue everyone."

"But you're not just anyone. I couldn't abandon you on the ridge, not without knowing why the crystal cut off."

"I understand, I do." He caressed her face, ending by tapping her chin to emphasize his words. "You don't always have to be the one to save me and our friends. Father Matt says it's not healthy for you."

"You've been talking with Matt about me?"

"Yes. We've discussed Anne-Louise's bite and my reaction to it." He paused, considering how to phrase the issue delicately. "Matt was concerned I was taking advantage of your instinct to rescue those you love."

Her fingers stroked his cheek. "You're not taking advantage of me."

"Still, if you keep trying to rescue everyone, the outcome isn't going to be good. Agathe wasn't happy with revealing what we are to Tig. Please, Cerissa, consider my words."

She sighed. "I— Yes, maybe I need to pull back on that urge. Or at least promise to try."

He kissed her gently. "We will both try."

"We've already made some progress, when you reflect on it. You let go of control enough to welcome Bear into our home, and I've agreed to let another instructor teach me how to pilot a private jet rather than insist we work together."

He chuckled. "I'll concede the point. I guess there are some compromises I'm willing to make because I love you."

"Me too, Quique. Me too."

CHAPTER 18

APOLOGIES

MOUNTAIN TOP CONDOS—A SHORT TIME LATER

Cerissa's stomach growled, and the rumbling sound forced her to move from the comfort of Henry's arms. "Could you please find my bathrobe? I'd like to go into the kitchen and see if Karen found anything worth eating."

He helped her into the fluffy white robe and put bunny slippers on her feet. She grabbed her contact lenses and slid them on, and he changed out of his grubby ski clothes. "I'll shower later. I want to make sure you're all right first."

Still weak, she leaned against him as they walked into the living room. She didn't regret for a moment her failed rescue attempt, even though Henry chastised her—or maybe because of that. They both loved each other deeply, and over the months they'd lived together, through the experiences they'd shared, they learned without artifice who the other was.

But she couldn't entirely ignore what he'd said. She had taken greater risks than called for last night, had rushed off too fast, not thinking it all through. She tried to save everyone, regardless of the cost to herself. She didn't know how she would change a habit that felt like an instinct, but she'd consider it for Henry. Despite how romantic his rescue had been, she didn't want that to become a pattern, either.

A clatter came from the kitchen. Karen puttered in the small space and dropped a metal spoon on a ceramic holder before closing the oven door with a *thump*. "If you're still hungry, I put some boneless chicken in the oven to bake and started a boxed stuffing mix cooking. When the buzzer goes off, could you turn off the stove and fluff the stuffing, Henry?"

"Of course," he replied.

"I'll be in the bedroom with Rolf. He's lying down and reading—his leg is still knitting together. He won't admit it, but he's in pain."

Cerissa considered offering him the clone blood she'd created, the one infused with a painkiller. But given Rolf's prior disgust over the idea, she didn't make the offer. Rolf was aware it existed, and if he wanted relief, he could ask.

See? She didn't always rescue everyone.

Henry guided her to the couch, where they could wait for the timer in comfort. She burrowed against him, only to feel Bear putting his paws on the sofa.

Henry pulled back and frowned. "The dog does not belong on furniture."

"Please? He's upset. He doesn't understand what happened to me."

"You are going to spoil him."

"Just like you spoil me."

"It's not the same."

"Henry."

He pursed his lips tightly, then his face softened. "Fine."

She helped Bear onto the couch, and he circled twice before settling next to her hip. Cerissa returned to snuggling against Henry.

"Now that you're injured, does that mean the skiing is done?" she asked.

"Yes."

"Then we can spend the evenings sightseeing. I flagged a couple of interesting art galleries on the Snowstone tourist app."

He puffed out a long-suffering breath, a noise she'd heard from him whenever he was about to do something he'd resisted doing. Usually to do with Anne-Louise.

"What would you say to arriving in New York a day early?" he asked.

Knew it.

She suppressed the self-satisfied smile she wanted to give and instead cocked her head. "I'm not against the idea, but why?"

"Well—"

Her spine snapped straight. The lenses she wore detected the microscopic changes. He was about to prevaricate. "Out with it, no omissions."

"Cerissa—"

"Something's been bothering you this whole trip. You've been irritable and angry. There's only one person who evokes that reaction in you with any regularity, but I couldn't guess why. And now you want to go to New York early. So, spit it out."

Henry growled, then sighed in resignation. "The reason Anne-Louise has been annoying me, tugging on the bond, was to compel me to interrupt our vacation and arrive early to attend the rehearsal dinner. When I refused to respond to her voicemails, she had Marcus contact me. That's how I lost my phone."

"You mean, that's when you smashed your phone against the rocks?"

He gave her a stern glare. "I refused to be at her beck and call. But now? Our skiing has been cut short anyway, so I am considering it. Begrudgingly."

Under the contract they'd signed, Anne-Louise was supposed to relinquish her claim on Henry's blood immediately. Using the maker-child bond to impose her wishes seemed to violate the spirit of that agreement. But taking legal action wasn't wise, either. Doing so would focus attention on Anne-Louise's original concern—that Cerissa wasn't mortal—and filing a complaint with the Collective wouldn't solve the immediate problem. According to Henry, there were only a few months left. By the time they resolved the matter in arbitration, the bond would have died.

Cerissa could never quite decide whether to treat Anne-Louise as a mother-in-law or an ex-wife. Maybe a strange combination of both? But either way, as Henry's maker, she would continue to be part of the family. "Then let's go to the rehearsal dinner. If Karen agrees."

"I thought you would say that."

"Wait. Is that why you didn't tell me before? Because you believed I'd insist on going?"

"Well—"

"Henry, aren't we further along than this? When a problem arises, you need to tell me right away."

"I just wanted time to consider it on my own. Anne-Louise is always difficult. I tire of it easily."

Yes, when Anne-Louise chose to, she could intentionally punch every one of Henry's buttons. Knowing someone as well and as long as his maker knew him gave her power to raise the annoyance factor quickly. "I understand. Still—"

"You're right. I should have told you from the start. I'm sorry."

The timer for the stuffing *buzzed*. Karen's bedroom door popped open. She emerged wearing a bathrobe and waved at them. "Stay there. I'll get it."

"Did Rolf tell you about the rehearsal dinner?" Cerissa asked.

"He did. He wants to go, since he can't ski while his leg mends." She set the stuffing pan on a trivet and poked it with a fork. "Besides, I think we should go, anyway. Weddings are special."

"Are you sure? It's one less day skiing—"

Karen grinned, looking like Bear with a fresh toy. "But an entire day shopping in New York? Are you kidding? I'll take that over skiing any day. I can't buy clothes in Mordida close to what the Manhattan shops carry. I'll find a gown for the Valentine's Day dance, and some outfits from the spring collection—"

"Okay, okay." Cerissa gestured for her friend to stop. "So you're voting yes. I concur. Henry?"

"As much as I hate giving in to Anne-Louise, it only makes sense."

"Then tomorrow, Karen and I can ski one last day together, and tomorrow night, you can fly us to New York."

"Sounds like a plan," Karen said, then ducked back into the bedroom, giving Cerissa a wink over her shoulder.

Cerissa decided not to pursue pilot training under the tutelage of Herr Müller. She would hire a non-vampire instructor with whom to continue her practice flights.

Maybe Henry would give her a lesson of a different kind, so they could become members of the mile-high club, too.

While the chicken finished baking, Cerissa had an idea, so she lifted her laptop from the end table and connected to the confidential Lux server. Something about the avalanche bothered her.

"What has that frown upon your face, *querida*?"

Typing in a few searches, she waited for the server to answer. "There'd been no warning of avalanches in the area before you guys left. You'd think mortals would be able to predict these things by now."

"It is not as easy as you suppose it to be."

She skimmed through the updated summary Lux scientists had prepared. "Hmm. We've noted an increase in avalanches due to wet storms, which create a lethal mix of rain and snow. It's filed under pending climate catastrophe. That sounds ominous."

"Indeed."

"And other impacts are noted—reduced harvest yields due to increased rains, continuing droughts in areas like Sierra Escondida, and ocean fish and tropical coral die-off from salination dilution when glaciers melt. Yikes. Predictions of reduced food production leading to mass starvation at some point in the next fifty years."

He pointed at the screen. "Click the link."

She did. And was instantly frustrated. "I don't have the necessary security clearance. I could call Ari—"

"There is nothing you can do about it right now. We are on vacation. When we return, ask him."

"How did I miss all this?" Her empty stomach clenched. This was awful on a global scale.

He squeezed her thigh. "It is easy to lose track of the bigger issues when you're living your life. And we've had enough trauma for one night. Is there something else you'd like to focus on? Something more pleasant?" He tried to close her laptop lid.

She stopped him and opened the wedding planner app instead. "Since we're grounded for the night, can we work on wedding plans?"

He grunted. "If we must."

"You make it sound like torture." She playfully slapped Henry's leg. "Don't you want to get married?"

"With all my heart. I merely hate the arguments that each decision will raise."

"Then let's start with the guestlist. I've filled in mine. Yours should be easy. Who do you want to invite?"

She handed him the laptop and pointed to the tab for the guestlist.

He raised his injured arm. "Um, perhaps you could type them in for me? It would be faster."

She took the laptop back. "Ready when you are."

She typed the names as he listed them, informing him when she'd already included a mutual friend. When he said, "Vishon Bathory," her fingers froze, hovering over the keyboard.

"No way."

"Why not? He's a councilman—"

"He's one of those mean vampires. The ones who accused me of awful things."

"I see. Is there a place for 'maybes' in the app?"

"There would need to be one for assholes to put his name down."

"Cerissa!"

She rolled her eyes at him, then studied the tabs on the planner app. Indeed, there was space for tentative invitations. "Here."

"Then we'll file him there and discuss the matter again later. If you decide you don't want him to attend, we won't invite him. I just want you prepared for the possibility someone brings him as a plus-one. You're friends with Haley."

Cerissa groaned. Haley had led the fight for mortal rights, and Cerissa had worked with her to get a mortal appointed to the town council. "Oh crap. I forgot about that. Fine. Invite him and Haley. See? I can compromise."

"As can I, or we would not be heading to New York early." Then he finished reciting names, and she typed in the rest of his list. "Are we having the wedding at home?" he asked.

"Karen offered her house. I like the idea. But she needs to ask Rolf first."

"Ask me what?"

Cerissa jumped, not realizing Rolf had re-emerged from Karen's bedroom. The oven buzzer went off again, and Karen rushed into the kitchen. "The chicken's ready to serve. I'll get it."

"What haven't you asked me, *Liebling*?"

"Oh. I thought we should offer them our house for the wedding. More room."

Rolf shrugged. "I have no problem with that. Being the best man, it only seems right."

"Best man?" Cerissa's stomach dipped. What if Henry didn't want Rolf as his best man? Would it cause a rift between the two friends? "Henry asked you already? He didn't tell me."

"Who else would he ask?"

"*Querida*, quit looking so worried. I asked him last night while we skied, before the avalanche hit."

"Oh." She pressed her hand against her chest. "That's a relief."

"And thank you, Rolf. We accept. So that takes care of location. Now we should discuss the budget."

"Karen and I need to shop caterers and florists first. And there's the sangeet party—"

Karen brought over a plate of roast chicken and stuffing, interrupting her. "Here you go."

"That looks great, thanks." Cerissa chewed a mouthful of stuffing, moaning as the savory soft bread melted on her tongue. Then she tried some of the chicken—her friend had seasoned it to perfection—and felt her energy returning as she ate.

Karen flopped down on one of the armchairs. "What's a sangeet party?"

"Lots of fun. Our families come together the day before the wedding to celebrate, and we do the mehendi ceremony then, with mehendi artists."

"Ah, translation, please?"

"The bride's hands and feet are decorated in intricate designs using henna dye, and guests at the sangeet can request a small design too. You'll love it—I'll show you photos later. Consider the party as similar to the American tradition of a rehearsal dinner, but more music and dancing and henna tattoos."

Henry *harrumphed*. "And the groom's family pays for that in America."

"Nope. I'm paying for half the sangeet party—you can pay the other half. And I'm paying for half the honeymoon too, and I'll accept no arguments from you. After this whole thing with Anne-Louise, you owe me."

"If I owe you, then shouldn't I pay for both?"

"It doesn't work that way. You don't get to choose your own punishment."

Henry let loose another long-suffering sigh.

From the bedroom doorway, Rolf whispered, "Puppy-whipped."

At hearing "puppy," Bear jumped off the couch, grasped the tug-of-war rope between his jaws, and trotted over to Rolf. He glared at the dog. "You think I'm going to play with you?"

Bear whined in response.

Cerissa laughed. "You're the one who woke him."

"All right." Rolf held on to the doorframe as he leaned over to grip the pull-handle. He whipped the blue rope from one side to the other as Bear hung onto the four-inch knot with his teeth, releasing and clamping his jaws again to cinch up the rope to grab Rolf's end. "But don't mistake me for her. You bite me, and I'll bite back."

CHAPTER 19
MORE WEDDING PLANS

NEW YORK CITY—THE NEXT NIGHT

An uneventful flight delivered them to La Guardia airport. Henry let Rolf pilot, and instead spent some delightful time with Cerissa in the plane's bedroom while Bear whined in the background. It wasn't even midnight by the time they arrived at the Collective's high rise. Arrangements had been made through Leopold, Cerissa's business partner, for each couple to have their own one-bedroom apartment on the guest floor.

The apartment Henry and Cerissa shared was the same one they'd stayed in for three weeks in December. He unpacked Bear's gear, creating a sleeping area for him in the kitchen, and, having already taken him for a pee break, put the pup to bed for the night. With all the social engagements planned, arrangements had been made to have pet-sitters care for the pup's needs whenever they weren't in the apartment.

Cerissa sat on the couch, working at her laptop. "Henry, why did you check the box that our wedding service will be non-religious?"

He hadn't realized she was working on wedding prep again. He'd filled in some more sections after she went to sleep last night, items that only required a mouse click to complete. "Since you were raised Hindu, but are Lux, and I'm Catholic, I assumed it would be best not to argue over which religious ceremony to use. We had a hard enough time with the guestlist, and there is still the budget to decide—"

"You see it as an argument. I see it as an opportunity to compromise. We include a little from each. I've already spoken to Father Matt, and he agreed to incorporate the Hindu aspects I want."

Henry joined her on the couch. "I never pictured you as religious—"

"Spiritual, not religious." She tilted her hand back and forth, gesturing ambivalence. "But I still enjoy traditions from my childhood. Yoga, meditation, ritual—especially the wedding rituals."

"Then we have that in common," he said. "I find peace in the Catholic rituals. And before I go to sleep, I either pray or meditate."

"Really?" Cerissa lifted her chin, surprise on her face. "You've been a bit hesitant to talk about your spiritual beliefs, which seems strange, considering we're engaged, but I was afraid to push."

His stomach churned. Money had already become a bone of contention at times, although that was more on his part than hers. He didn't want religion to become a source of disagreement either. "I wasn't sure how you would feel about my religious practices."

"I guess it depends. I don't see anything innately wrong with prayer, as long as you're not focused on doing ill toward your competitors or enemies."

"No, my prayers are not of that nature."

"What do you pray for?"

He looked out the sliding glass balcony door at the infinite winter sky, the high-rise buildings surrounding them dusted with snow, icicles hanging from window frames, and made his decision. "I will tell you, but you must not judge me harshly for it."

"I don't understand."

They'd been together almost a year, and she'd never criticized his confession appointments with Father Matt. In fact, she'd been supportive, going to Christmas mass with him. Why his sudden fear?

Henry turned back to her and took her hand, rubbing his fingers over hers. "I sometimes wonder if you see us as a primitive culture, if you would see prayer as a meaningless superstition."

"You're afraid that's how I view your Catholicism?"

He nodded.

"I have my disagreements with some of the practices of the Catholic Church, but that doesn't mean I think you're wrong or primitive for being Catholic. And I've seen for myself that confession helps you be a better person. When you pray, what do you pray for?"

"Do you really want to know?"

"Yes, I do. I want to learn all about you. I'm surprised you didn't raise your concern before this."

"Well, now I'm safe. I have you well and truly trapped as my fiancée." He slid his good arm around her and pulled her close to him. "You can't leave."

She chuckled and kissed his cheek. "Then it's about time you tell me."

He half shrugged and released her. "To answer your question, when I pray, I pray for answers."

"You mean, you ask a question?"

"Sometimes. Sometimes it is as general as asking God how I can be a better person, in spite of what I am." Although he didn't often discuss his struggles with her, the reality of being vampire, of becoming a monster, weighed on him. "Sometimes, I ask whether I should do something or not. Such as the night of the horseback ride, when the assassin shot you, and you stayed at my house for the first time. When I got on my knees to pray that morning..."

"You kneel to pray?"

"Yes, unless I'm not alone. When Rolf and I bunk together, I do not kneel. It would make him uncomfortable."

"I see."

"As I was saying, when I prayed that morning, I asked God whether I should believe your story about being Lux. I woke the next evening feeling confident that believing you was the right thing to do."

"I'm glad that's the answer you got. Very glad." She quirked her head to the side. "So you don't ask for things? Or to have events go your way?"

"No. I was taught as a child by the priests that such prayers would be selfish. God is not here to give us what we presume we want. When I was first turned, I would pray, asking whether I should destroy myself. I feared I'd become this evil, vile thing that God would want destroyed. But no answer ever came."

"Perhaps no answer is an answer."

"Perhaps."

"I'm glad you have a spiritual practice that helps you."

That was not the response he was expecting. "You do not think less of me for seeking guidance from God?"

"No. As long as I've known you, you've seemed to get a lot from Father Matt's counsel."

"I assumed you'd conclude I was being superstitious to believe that God gives me guidance."

She didn't answer him. Instead, she unbuttoned the top button of his shirt, lifted the crucifix that he wore, and ran her finger over the hard body of Jesus still nailed to the cross. "Why do you wear this?"

"As a symbol of my faith," Henry replied.

"I have studied world religions and have never understood why Christians focus on the instrument of torture that brought his death."

"It is a reminder of his sacrifice, for our sins." He took the cross from her, kissed it, and tucked it under his shirt. "Now do you think me superstitious?"

"Henry, I don't judge you over your religious beliefs."

"But you do have an opinion."

"As I said, I've studied many religions, and try as I do, I don't get the same meaning out of Christ's death that Christians do."

"What meaning do you take from it?"

"Let's postulate for a moment that your basic premise is true. That God is something separate from us, that he or she incarnated as human."

"Go on."

"So God sets up this plan, where he is killed as the sacrificial lamb, to rise from the dead and cleanse mankind of its sins, just by believing in him?"

"There is more to it than that," Henry said. "But you have the basics."

"Remember, you asked."

He felt her stiffen in his arms. Was she girding herself for war? "And that would be?"

She huffed out a reluctant-sounding breath. "God didn't plan his death that way, nor could he have stopped it if he wanted to—he cried out, 'Why have you forsaken me?' for a reason. He experienced the alienation that humans feel at the moment of their death, endured the cruelty of man against man, and was powerless to prevent tragic results. It's like all the other inhumane things humans do to each other. The wars, the pogroms, the Spanish Inquisition, the Crusades, the witch burnings, the Nazi death camps—all these hideously horrible acts, God is unable to stop them, even when they violate his...or her...commandments. God is not all-powerful. God cannot act separately from the physical laws of this world. God is in and of this world, but not outside of it. God's sole power is in the voluntary compliance of human beings—when they collectively act out of love to choose a different path than pain and suffering."

"But the resurrection? He overcame death and bodily rose to heaven. It wiped away our sins, our fears."

"All human fear is fear of dying," she replied. "Human psychology is such that humans cannot contemplate their own death." She paused. "Henry, I don't mean to challenge your beliefs. You're entitled to them, as long as you don't use them to harm others with them. But he was not the first to resurrect. Lazarus was also raised from the dead. Why did his death not have the same meaning?"

"So you think I'm wrong to believe?"

"I'm not talking about what you believe, so much as what I believe, what I've seen over the years. My belief? When you pray, you're connecting to your inner godhood—you're accessing your higher self, which is connected with all the other higher selves constituting what humans call God. The psychologist, Carl Jung, called it the collective unconscious. He was onto something when he named it."

"An interesting angle." He'd read enough to have encountered others who believed as she did. But she still hadn't answered his question. "Do you think Christianity is wrong?"

"You're not going to let me avoid your question, are you?"

"I would like to hear your answer."

"You are aware that the early Christian church struggled with the dualism of whether doing good acts or preaching the word was the key to their beliefs?"

"It's both."

"I lean more to assessing people by their acts, not their words. If humans followed the simple admonition to love your neighbor as yourself, then much of what's wrong with this world would be cured. And 'when you do this for the least of these my brothers, you do them to me.' He acknowledged the divinity of every person—that the god-self dwells within each human, and that honoring it is the same as honoring God. If you examine other religions, you'll find similar ethical teachings running through them as well. Truths that seem to transcend religious boundaries."

She stopped talking. Henry remained silent as well.

"Knowing my perspective," she finally said, "does it change how you feel about me?"

He was a bit surprised by the question. He'd always been concerned that she would be the one to judge him harshly for his faith. "I always knew you were not Christian, *querida*. I do not love you any less to know why. And if you had to pick anything from my religious beliefs to hold up as truths, I am glad you picked the ones that you did." He kissed her cheek softly. "Besides," he added, breaking into a big smile, "I have hundreds of years to convert you."

She slapped his arm softly, laughing. "That works both ways, Quique. Just remember. I have the same opportunity to convert you."

CHAPTER 20

PROBLEM SOLVED

The apartment doorbell rang, and Henry greeted the delivery person, examining the clothing in the plastic bag. His suit and shirt had come back pressed to perfection by the Collective's laundry service. He would reserve the tux for Anne-Louise's wedding. Through a little Lux magic, Cerissa flashed to their house to gather an extra change of formalwear for the rehearsal party once they finished their own wedding planning.

And after their discussion of religious beliefs, he'd agreed their ceremony could be a blended one with elements from both traditions.

He returned to the bedroom, dressed, and slipped the necktie off the hanger.

"Let me help you." Cerissa took the silver and blue striped tie from his hand and hooked it around his neck. He watched her in the mirror as she tied a perfect full Windsor knot. "Did you tell Anne-Louise?"

"That we would attend the rehearsal and dinner? Yes."

"No, I mean what happened to your arm." She carefully pushed back his sleeve and peeled away the beige elastic sock, one specially designed for an amputee, revealing the fresh growth. "The wrist stub looks healthy. By tomorrow night, the base of your hand should have regrown."

He pulled the sock back into place and adjusted the cuff link. She had purchased the sock in Colorado at his request—without the covering, the new skin itched annoyingly. "You don't have to keep checking it."

"I'm just concerned—and curious. I'm logging the progress each day, to add to my observations."

His beautiful mate could never let go of her scientific curiosity when it came to vampires. But he wouldn't tolerate any distractions. "Tonight, you are my date, and not a scientist."

She gave him a self-satisfied grin. "I'm always both." She raised a finger and stalled his response. "After misbehaving and hiding the reason behind your tug-of-war with Anne-Louise, you don't get the last word tonight."

He bowed, conceding to her wisdom. After all, she was right. This time.

How long would he let her use that particular excuse to get her way? Maybe a little longer, and then he'd put his foot down.

Father Matt called it setting a boundary.

Henry preferred the old-fashioned term better.

"Are you sure you want to attend the rehearsal dinner?" he asked her.

"Gladly." Cerissa hooked his right arm with hers. "We're one step closer to getting Anne-Louise married off."

The Collective's wedding chapel was gorgeous, and reminded Cerissa of the chapels one might see on a luxury cruise liner in the early 1920s. Heavy, dark wood paneling inset with tall, rectangular stained glass, and each faux window artificially lit from behind to glow. The center aisle led to a small altar and rail in hardwood, matching the paneling.

Still holding Henry's arm, she stood quietly with him in the narthex, waiting for everyone to gather for the rehearsal. When her cousin strolled through the doorway, she shot him a look.

What was Ari doing here? He wasn't part of the wedding party. How did he learn about the rehearsal dinner? Not that Ari ever refused a free feed.

He answered the unvoiced question. "The groom invited me. I'm handling tech for the wedding reception and sitting on his side. Tig told him about my involvement in his rescue. I guess that makes me family."

"I should have known you'd wangle an invitation."

"I wasn't the only one. So did Tig, but she declined. Too much time off the Hill."

Cerissa crossed her arms and raised a brow, mimicking a stance she'd often seen Henry take. "Did Gaea come with you?"

"She passed. Hates traveling on planes. Something about newfangled contraptions that fall from the sky."

More people entered the narthex, gathering in small groups. A couple of female vampires Cerissa hadn't met huddled together—bridesmaids, perhaps. The two men—both mortals—were probably Rick's groomsmen. One man about Rick's age communicated through sign language with a younger woman.

Cerissa made an educated guess: they were Rick's brother and sister.

"Do you know everyone here?" she asked Ari.

"No, but I plan to before the weekend's over."

"Ari!" She slapped his chest, aghast. "What about Gaea?"

"I told you already: we have a happily open relationship."

"You're incorrigible, you know?"

He waggled his eyebrows. "So is she. It's great."

"Yes, but it would have been nice if you'd answered the phone when Henry called you from Colorado."

"Does Henry pick up the phone when he's in your bed?"

Cerissa conceded the battle and shrugged at him.

"I called Karen later, but she was already on her way to collect you both."

"She told me," Cerissa grumbled at him. "But you're still incorrigible."

Ari laughed.

Anne-Louise arrived on Rick's arm fashionably late, and she instantly zeroed in on Henry.

"Where is your hand?" his maker demanded.

"Missing in action."

"Whatever happened?"

Ari squeezed in between them before Henry answered. "Fingernail biting. Bad habit. He needs to give it up."

"A recent skiing accident." Henry moved Ari aside and rolled back the sleeve to reveal the elastic bandage-like sock. Then he leaned toward his maker and whispered, "It should fully regrow in a few days."

Anne-Louise scoffed. "But you'll wreck the wedding pictures."

Henry huffed, and the crystal sent an icy blast Cerissa's way, communicating his anger. They'd embedded the crystal in his regrown wrist last night, and he hadn't worn the muting bracelet tonight. The crystal needed time unencumbered to reconnect them. The process appeared successful, if the icy blast was any sign.

Anne-Louise scowled, acting as if Henry had misplaced the hand on purpose to spoil her wedding. Rick tried to shush her, to no avail, then rolled his eyes. Cerissa couldn't wait to see Henry's maker married off and officially Rick's problem instead of theirs.

"I can hide my arm behind Cerissa's back," Henry finally offered.

"No, that will not do! How do I walk down the aisle on your arm with, with"—she gestured frantically—"with no arm?"

Ow. Gooseflesh shot over Cerissa's skin. After they'd arrived early at his maker's insistent request, being chastised in front of everyone ramped his rage even higher. But aside from the gusting chill sent her way, he seemed to contain it—mostly.

He growled. "I have an arm. I don't have a hand. And you can walk on my right."

Rick's brother signed furiously in American Sign Language, giving his sister a blow-by-blow of the argument. Cerissa had to suppress her laughter. The exaggerated gestures and facial expressions he made, similar to a dancer's movements, nailed Anne-Louise's attitude to a T.

She couldn't begin to imagine what the mortals thought of Anne-Louise's callous words. Of course, they weren't aware the hand would soon regrow.

"Is Mother giving you a hard time?" Chen Méi asked with a smirk, joining the battle. "I can walk on her right."

According to a text Rick sent Cerissa, he'd told his mortal relatives that Chen Méi and Henry were adopted children from a prior marriage.

"Thank you, daughter. While I appreciate your thoughtfulness, his empty sleeve will hang at his side. It'll ruin the pictures."

Cerissa stepped forward, concerned that if this went on much longer, Henry's rage would implode, and she'd be frozen by the artic blast. "I could buy a prothesis for him during the day, and if he wore gloves, no one would know the difference." Then she looked over at the mortals. "The doctor will fit him with a lifelike robotic hand when we return home."

It was best to cover all their bases. She wasn't sure if they'd see Rick's family in some other context in the future, but they might.

"It will have to do," Anne-Louise said. "If he'll agree to wear the hand."

Henry bowed. "If it will make Cerissa happy, I will do so." He trailed his fingers along her back. "I'll do anything to make her happy."

Cerissa sighed and leaned into him. The next wedding they'd attend would be their own, and it couldn't happen soon enough for her. Yes, they occasionally had misunderstandings, but then, every couple did. It was how they resolved them that mattered.

And she trusted Henry, deep in her heart, to find his way back to her no matter who or what stirred his anger. Because his love for her, and her love for him, was all they needed to steer a peaceful course together.

In that, she had every confidence.

CHAPTER 21
MARRIAGE VOWS

THE COLLECTIVE BALLROOM—THE NEXT NIGHT

The rehearsal finished with no further problems. The only surprise Henry faced at the ceremony was Anne-Louise's elaborate wedding gown. The white dress had multi-ringed side hoops—panniers, as they were called back in the day—that supported the sideways-jutting skirt modeled on the dresses of the eighteenth century. To avoid treading on the draped silk taffeta, he stepped carefully while escorting her down the aisle with Méi on her other side.

Before they started, his sister eyed the dress and wisecracked about Mother living in the Dark Ages. He wisely kept his lips sealed.

Once the wedding finished, and the photographer was done, Henry offered Cerissa his arm, leading her to the reception ballroom. He navigated between the round tables, which were draped in white linens. Centerpieces featuring blood-red orchids sat on each table, the orchids' lips showing a touch of cream in their centers. After hunting around, they finally found table number ten.

Rolf and Karen would join them shortly. At the moment, Rolf was working the room with Karen at his side, making new business contacts and solidifying those they already had with members of the Collective.

A lone man sat at table number ten, a glass of red wine in his hand, his back to them, wavy, dark brown hair to his collar, and broad shoulders filling his suit coat. *Ari.* From the scent wafting Henry's way, the glass held the reserve wine Cerissa had brought as a wedding gift and was indeed being served tonight.

Henry pulled out the chair next to Ari. "Cerissa, would you like to sit by your cousin?"

"Sure." She gracefully slid onto the seat, smoothing her sleek navy-blue formal dress over her sexy butt as she eased down. Her mink-brown hair was braided elaborately with pearls that trailed across her neck in a circle, and a matching pearl comb holding it halfway up.

He couldn't help but admire his gorgeous mate.

When he took the chair next to her, she said, "A beautiful ceremony. Rick seemed so happy."

"Indeed." Henry extended his arm with the fake hand. "Now that the wedding is over, and the photos finished, may I remove this monstrosity?"

"I don't see why not." She started to push the sleeve up his forearm.

"Wait. Let me take off the tuxedo coat first. I don't want it wrinkled."

With a shake of her head, Cerissa smirked.

Too bad. He cared about his appearance. It showed his respect for her that he didn't want his clothes to look like he'd slept in them. Once the coat was off, and his cuff link removed, he rolled the shirt sleeve carefully to avoid wrinkling it until he revealed his wrist, which was wrapped in leather straps holding on the prothesis.

There. That would do.

Cerissa got to work unfastening the harness. Once the straps were off, her nimble fingers rolled back the cuplike cushioned protector made of silicone that hugged his wrist. Then she helped him slip a protective sock over the new skin growth.

Now finished, he shook his arm to rid himself of the skin-crawling shiver the suction cup left behind and unfolded his shirt sleeve. He fastened the cuff link and slipped the tuxedo coat back on. "That feels better, thank you."

She offered him the hand. "What should I do with this?"

"Trash it. I will never use it again."

"That's wasteful. Maybe I can donate it."

She placed it on the table.

"No." He scooped up the prosthetic and tucked it out of sight in his lap. What a breach of etiquette to put such a thing on the table where others would eat.

"Hey, kiddos," Ari said. "I'll take it to my room. Be back in a flash."

Henry passed the hand over, and Ari headed to the elevator lobby.

"I hope he doesn't literally mean flash—"

"Henry! Cerissa! What are you doing here?" Allison's voice shouldn't have surprised him, but it did. His ex-girlfriend now worked as one of Leopold's envoys.

He stood and gave a slight bow. "Anne-Louise asked me to walk her down the aisle, along with Méi. Didn't you see us enter together?"

"Sorry, we arrived late for the ceremony. I had to work today, and rushed to get ready."

"Well, you look lovely. And hello, Warren." Henry offered his uninjured hand, and they shook.

Warren sucked in his cheeks, uncertainty in his expression. "No hard feelings?"

He'd punched Henry—and accidentally hit Cerissa—to avenge Allison. But they'd made amends weeks ago. "We are past that. All is fine."

"Good, because Anne-Louise put us at your table."

Henry groaned. Leave it to his maker to find another way to torment him and stir the pot. "If this is too awkward, we could ask someone to swap with you."

Allison's arm linked with Warren's. "It's okay. Warren has been helping me adjust." She smiled, glowing, at the chief security officer. "We're dating. We had a lovely Christmas. I introduced him to my parents by videoconference."

"I am happy for you both."

"Yeah, wish we could have done it in person, but I'm low on the seniority pole and had to work Christmas day at CNT. But I had Christmas night off." She grinned again at Warren. "We're mated now."

Henry didn't inquire, but he could imagine. By the way Allison made eyes at Warren, the couple had probably consummated the relationship that night. Henry was glad she had adjusted to vampires and found someone worthy of her.

"Congratulations." He gestured to the empty seats across from them. "And please, have a seat."

Waiters served the meal and brought a glass of alcohol-spiked blood disguised as a Bloody Mary to each vampire present. A small party from Rick's family—mortals who weren't aware of the secret—were seated at their own table on one side of the room close to the head table. Henry suspected the surrounding tables of mortals-in-the-know and vampires from the Collective would ensure Rick's family didn't see anything that would give away the secret existence of vampires—or if they did catch an inadvertent peek, a vampire would be drafted to mesmerize them to forget.

While the plates were being cleared away, Leopold ambled over and greeted them. Then he said, "Cerissa, my dear, you've been holding out on me."

Still sitting, she scrunched her brows at him. "Whatever do you mean?"

Leopold waved a tall glass with ice, a hint of red, and a telltale celery stalk. "Why didn't you tell me you developed clone blood with alcohol?"

"I did. It's in the reports I've sent you. Not to mention we served it at the engagement party."

Leopold *harrumphed*. "Well, you'll have to send me a case a week."

"A case a month. We still aren't at full production yet."

"Two cases a month."

"One. Take it or leave it. Nothing in our deal said I had to produce it."

Leopold laughed. "You are a tough bargainer. Fine. One case a month, for now. But once the lab is built—"

"Now, Leopold, we're at Anne-Louise's wedding." Cerissa exhaled a loud breath. "Enough with business. Why don't you get yourself another drink and relax?"

Henry had been about ready to jump in and intervene. Fortunately, her sponsor took the hint and left. After the dancing started, Henry found himself alone at the table with Cerissa. "You know what we forgot to do in the bite contract with Anne-Louise?" he asked.

Cerissa sipped her wine before answering. "What's that?"

"The house I'm required to build for my maker's use when she visits the Hill. We should have insisted she nullify the obligation, since she will no longer have a need for it."

Cerissa returned her glass to the table, looking thoughtful. "I didn't want to cancel it. In a hundred years, we'll be glad we have the extra room."

Henry's eyebrows spiked. "Why in a hundred years?"

She glanced around, perhaps checking to make sure no one else had heard. "Remember how I told you the Lux banded me and kept me in human form as a child, not allowing me to morph?"

"I recall."

"Well, I'm not doing that to my children. But it also means I'll need a lot of help to monitor them. Can't allow the little ones to morph into a rabbit or dog and get lost. Lux *karabu*—those who are in their intermediate stage—can serve as nannies and mannies. They'll live in the extra guest house." Cerissa gave him a shrewd smile. "We never promised Anne-Louise the house would only be for her. Just that she could stay there when visiting. Doubt she will with babies in residence."

A warmth grew in his chest, and he toasted her with his Bloody Mary glass. His beautiful fiancée had planned ahead for their future family.

What else might she be plotting that she hadn't told him yet?

He shook his head. It didn't matter. He'd find out when she was ready to tell him. "How was dinner?"

"Wonderful. The caterer did a splendid job pairing each course with the perfect wine selection."

"Have you decided what sort of meal we'll serve at our reception?"

"Karen and I are going to talk with the caterers when we return home. But I'm not choosing the cuisine alone. You and I are. Together."

"Of course, *mi amor*." He pushed his chair back. "Would you like to dance?"

She blotted her mouth with the napkin then set it beside her empty plate. "I'd love to. I need to burn some energy. There's cake soon."

He laughed. He expected the cake to be of the same quality as the dinner, and for her, he was glad. She loved her sweets.

As they entered the dance floor, he pondered the question. What kind of cake would she pick for their wedding? Knowing her, it would have chocolate in it. And he'd take one bite to make her happy. Of the cake, that was. Biting her would come after the ceremony, when all the guests were gone.

The band played a slow love ballad. Henry swept her into his arms, holding her close with his partial arm resting against her back. He'd be pleased when his hand finished growing back in. There were things he enjoyed doing in bed that required all his fingers.

"Whatever are you thinking about?" she asked.

"You."

"I know that tone. Well, hold your thought for a while. We aren't leaving the reception early. I'm enjoying dancing with you." She kissed his cheek. "Oh, question. Why did they do a blood ritual as part of the ceremony? The officiant did a nice job of hiding the fact they were sharing blood, but will we have to?"

"They combined the engagement ritual you and I have already completed with their wedding ceremony. There was such a short time between the engagement and the wedding, they did both at once."

Backstage before the ceremony, he'd witnessed the officiant draw blood from Rick and Anne-Louise and mix it into a gold goblet. The language of the pledge had been slightly modified to cover the fact uninitiated mortals were in the audience.

"That's a relief," Cerissa said. "I don't want to become vampire in front of thirty Hill vampires in order to drink your blood. They might notice the change."

"Never fear. There's no need. And I spoke with Father Matt last night. He's been reading up on Hindu traditions and sounds very enthusiastic."

"Oh goodie. Karen and I have planned the design of the *mandapa* already."

Last night, she'd shown him a photo of the four-pillar structure. It was open on top with flower garlands over the support pillars and the lateral rails, similar to the chuppah Shayna and Yacov were married under, but without the canopy of the chuppah.

"What other traditions do you want?"

"The center fire to watch us. We won't have parents under the *mandapa*—yours are no longer with us, and only my mother is alive. To avoid awkwardness, we'll skip that. But besides our rings, I want to do an exchange of floral garlands and tying our garments together. We'll have to decide what you'll wear for the tying."

"Perhaps a tuxedo scarf?"

"That might work."

The slow dance continued, and he leaned in closer, his cheek against hers.

"What about you?" she asked. "What from the Catholic wedding ceremony do you want included?"

"I'm not sure. Perhaps the Eucharist? Perhaps in our vows?"

"And what vows would those be?"

"Oh, the usual. You'll promise to *love, honor, and obey* me."

She pulled back and laughed. Loudly. "You are a dreamer, aren't you?"

"What? Why not?"

"When do I ever obey you?"

He stared into her beautiful emerald eyes, which sparkled with her mirth, and his lips curled up at the corners. "When it's my turn to choose."

She ducked her face into the crook of his neck, and her skin blushed so hot he felt the passionate heat rise as they danced cheek to cheek.

A NOTE FROM JENNA

Thank you for reading *Dark Wine at Christmas*. I hope you enjoyed it!

The adventure for Henry and Cerissa and their friends continues in Book 11 of the Hill Vampire series, *Dark Wine at the Altar*.

Are you ready for a wedding? I'm still trying to figure out what I'll wear...

As Cerissa and Henry step up to the altar to get married, will they really have a happily ever after?

With threats following them from their home to their honeymoon, Cerissa must face the truth: she can't save everyone.

Want to be among the first to receive updates about new releases, along with special announcements, exclusive excerpts, and other free fun stuff? Join Jenna Barwin's VIP Readers at jennabarwin.com.

Hate newsletters? Then follow me on BookBub:

https://www.bookbub.com/authors/jenna-barwin

And be sure to subscribe to author alerts to receive a notice when new books are released. BookBub won't send an alert unless you subscribe to "author alerts"—you may want to confirm you're subscribed.

Happy reading!
Jenna Barwin

P.S. To an author, reviews are better than dark wine!

ACKNOWLEDGMENTS AND DEDICATIONS

To my husband Eric— thank you for inspiring many of the doggie shenanigans. Your love of dogs has rubbed off on me. Love you!

To Sharon Bonin Pratt for your generous help as an early reader, pointing out ways to improve the story.

To Caitlyn O'Leary—thank you for your help with critiquing my cover designs and your all-around encouragement. Always appreciated!

To my editing team—it takes a team to polish a story and ready it for readers. Katrina, Trenda, and Arran—you are all fantastic! You push me to make the story better, and I sincerely appreciate it.

Any errors in grammar, clarity, or plot are mine, not theirs. Their full names are:

- Katrina Diaz-Arnold, Refine Editing, LLC
- Trenda K. Lundin, It's Your Story Content Editing
- Arran McNicol, Editing 720

In particular, thank you Katrina for suggesting I make this story a separate book rather than include it in *Dark Wine at Dawn*. Doing so made it a much fuller tale and really sets us up for Henry and Cerissa's wedding.

And thank you to my award-winning cover designer, Christian Bentulan with Covers by Christian. As always, he did an outstanding job on the cover design.

There are many other wonderful people who have helped me improve my writing, and also advised me on tackling the business of being a writer. The generosity of other writers, who have freely shared their expertise, is greatly appreciated. Thank you everyone for your support and guidance!

Printed in Great Britain
by Amazon

42241204R00098